MURDER ON THE FILM
THE COMPLETE CASES OF
CANDID JONES, VOLUME 1

BOOKS IN THE ARGOSY LIBRARY:

MURDER ON
THE FILM

THE COMPLETE CASES OF
CANDID JONES, VOLUME 1

RICHARD B. SALE

ILLUSTRATED BY
JOSEPH A. FARREN

POPULAR PUBLICATIONS · 2025

© 2025 Popular Publications, an imprint of Steeger Properties, LLC

First Edition—2025

PUBLISHING HISTORY

"Long Shot" originally appeared in the January 9, 1937 issue of *Detective Fiction Weekly* magazine (Vol. 107, No. 6). Copyright © 1937 by The Frank A. Munsey Company. Copyright renewed © 1964 and assigned to Steeger Properties, LLC. All rights reserved.

"Neat But Not Gaudy" originally appeared in the January 30, 1937 issue of *Detective Fiction Weekly* magazine (Vol. 108, No. 3). Copyright © 1937 by The Frank A. Munsey Company. Copyright renewed © 1964 and assigned to Steeger Properties, LLC. All rights reserved.

"Murder on the Film" originally appeared in the April 3, 1937 issue of *Detective Fiction Weekly* magazine (Vol. 109, No. 6). Copyright © 1937 by The Frank A. Munsey Company. Copyright renewed © 1964 and assigned to Steeger Properties, LLC. All rights reserved.

"One Herring—Very Red" originally appeared in the May 1, 1937 issue of *Detective Fiction Weekly* magazine (Vol. 110, No. 4). Copyright © 1937 by The Frank A. Munsey Company. Copyright renewed © 1964 and assigned to Steeger Properties, LLC. All rights reserved.

"Flash!" originally appeared in the May 29, 1937 issue of *Detective Fiction Weekly* magazine (Vol. 111, No. 2). Copyright © 1937 by The Frank A. Munsey Company. Copyright renewed © 1964 and assigned to Steeger Properties, LLC. All rights reserved.

Visit ARGOSYMAGAZINE.COM for more books like this.

TABLE OF CONTENTS

LONG SHOT

Meet Candid Jones, Two-Fisted Camera-Toting Ex-Dick, Who Comes back to Play a Fast, Deadly Game against a Gang of Race-Track Smartsters!

1

THE VANISHING JOCKEY

IT WAS ABOUT three-thirty on a Thursday afternoon in September, and I had just hung up a roll of 35mm negatives to dry on the rack when there was a knock at the studio door and I said: "Come in."

The door opened and a girl entered. She closed the door casually behind her and then smiled at me and said: "Hello!"

I looked at her. She was young and she was beautiful. She had a skin like peaches and cream and her hair was in a long bob, ash-blond, and topped by a crazy little gray turban with a small impertinent veil. Her gray shoes were expensive, her gray coat more so.

I said: "You're not the model I asked the Acme Agency to send up?"

"I've been told I photograph very well," she answered.

I nodded. "Like a million bucks, no doubt. But you're not the model."

"No," she said. "I'm not the model. I'm looking for some one I used to know." She cocked her head to one side and stared at me casually. "The red hair is the same. So is the nose."

"What is this, lady?" I asked, annoyed.

"But you've got more freckles," she said. "And I think you've gotten thinner."

"Get to the point," I said. "If you're looking for a job, you've got one. I can use a type like you."

"Uh-uh," she said. "I'm not looking for a job. I'm trying to hire some one myself."

"Me?"

"I don't know. The man I want is named Terrence Jones. People used to call him Candid. He always said what he thought candidly. He used a gun and his fists the same way."

She had me going. I frowned at her. "My name is Candid Jones," I said.

"But not the same one." She shook her head sadly. "The one I want used to be the best damn detective the Apex Insurance Company—or any other insurance company for that matter—ever had. That was before his hobby made a sissy of him. You see, he used to be crazy to take pictures. He was a little warped on the subject. He used to carry a candid camera around with him wherever he went and he'd shoot everything he could see. And then one day he decided to give up sleuthing and take up photography as a business instead. It made him a sissy."

"It made him a lot of rocks," I said, smiling. "Who are you anyway? I can't place the face, but you're kind of fresh, and that's familiar."

"He was a good detective," she said.

"Who told you?" I grinned at her.

"I'm an eye-witness," she said. She sat down opposite my desk and I sat down behind it and gave her a cigarette and we both lighted up. "You see—four years ago—in 1932

I told the little Jockey
what to do. Lives and
a couple of fortunes
depended on him

it was, my mother was robbed of two hundred thousand dollars worth of jewels while she was staying at the Bay Towers Hotel in Miami Beach. These jewels were insured by Apex. They sent their best man down to recover them—Candid Jones. He had the jewels and the culprits back in four days. I never forgot that."

I had her then. It had taken a long time but I had her. You couldn't blame me for not lamping her at first because she'd changed. It's easy to remember a mature face. But hers hadn't been mature when Mrs. Myron Benefield went through that Miami Beach heist. For Polly was only seventeen then and pretty much a kid. Four years!

"Polly," I said, "it's been a long time. How are you?"

She gasped, then leaned forward and laid her hand on my wrist. "Candid—you do remember me then?"

"Sure," I said. "Fresh kid, boyish bob. Kind of kill-simple. Wanted to know all the gruesome details of sudden death...."

"Was I that bad?" She laughed. But the laugh faded quickly and she bit her lip. "Why did you leave it?"

"I'm doing well, Polly," I said. "I get more kick out of photography! Why, do you know—"

She shook her head. "Don't you miss it at all?"

I SMILED AND shrugged. "Sometimes I do, frankly. Sometimes when I read in the paper about a rat or two pulling a job or a killing and getting away with it—I feel like going back. But gumshoe work wasn't nice, Polly. It's no fun."

She looked crushed. She bit her lip and let her head droop and then she said in a small voice: "You'll never go back then?"

"Not for a million fish," I said.

"For a friend?"

And suddenly the whole atmosphere was electric. I didn't say anything for a moment. I watched her and I could see that she'd paled and she was breathing quickly. I ground out my cigarette in an ash tray. "Maybe for a friend," I said. "It's not good being wound up like a watch spring, kid. Go ahead and cry if it'll make you feel better. I don't mind."

Just like that, she buried her face in her hands and burst into tears. She cried steadily and quietly for about three minutes, and then she dried her eyes and straightened up, took a breath, smiled wistfully. "I'm a fool," she said. "But I feel much better, Candid. I've been so frightened—"

I nodded. "Let's hear it."

"Candid—you've *got* to find Johnny Lister!"

"Who is Johnny Lister?"

"He's a jockey. He's disappeared!"

I lighted another cigarette. "Look, Polly. You don't make too much sense. Maybe you'd better start at the beginning."

Polly Benefield set her chin. "You're right. It begins back at Hialeah Park, Miami, Candid. I own a racing stable, you know."

"I didn't."

"Yes. Mother bought it for me. You've read about it. The Benefield Stud."

"Oh. Go on."

"I have twelve horses, Candid. But my favorite is Bojangles. I raised her myself. She's a black beauty, really, and I love her. She—"

"Bojangles!" I said. "I won a century on that nag when she took the cup in the Brooke Handicap at Hialeah. I didn't know she was your horse!"

Polly smiled. "Yes, she's all mine." Her face clouded abruptly. "You remember, there was another horse in that race—Lampoon, the favorite. He belonged to Mr. John Hedwick. Bojangles beat him."

"Yes?"

"Well, Mr. Hedwick and I have been friendly rivals all the way. After that race he came around and made a wager with me on which was the better horse, Lampoon or my own Bojangles. We decided that the horse which won two out of three races in which they both were matched would win the wager."

"How much?" I asked.

"Oh, it's only a thousand dollars," Polly said. "We really put money on it to make it exciting. Then we went to Pimlico. And there, Lampoon beat Bojangles out in the

Arlington Classic. That made it even—both horses with one race."

"Keep talking," I said.

"Finally we wound up at Fairview Park for the Advance Guard Handicap on Saturday. This is the one which will decide the bet. Mr. Hedwick and I were both very thrilled. It's—well—you've no idea what sport it is to watch those two horses race—"

"And what's happened?"

"TWO DAYS AGO," she said, "Johnny Lister came to me. He's Bojangles' rider. He told me that he'd been approached by two men and offered ten thousand dollars if he'd *pull* Bojangles in the Advance Guard Handicap."

"Good kid," I said. "What did he tell them?"

"He told them no," Polly said. "But he said he thought he should tell me to have another jockey—some one I could trust—ready for the race in case anything happened to him."

I didn't say anything.

"That was Tuesday. I haven't seen him nor had a word from him since. Candid—please—you've got to find that boy for me. It's not the race. I don't care if Bojangles even runs it. But I'm afraid something has happened to Johnny!"

"This Mr. Hedwick of yours," I said, "he wouldn't be so damned cracked to win this race with Lampoon that he'd try to buy your jockey into throwing it?"

Polly looked horrified. "Lord no, Candid! He's in this—" she stopped. "Last night, somebody tried to kill Lampoon—shoot him—"

"Tell me."

"Nobody seems to know. Lampoon's trainer—Old

Whitey—heard some one fiddling with the stable door. He got up and saw a man with a gun. He yelled, the man fired at Lampoon, then hit Whitey over the head and knocked him out and fled. The bullet missed Lampoon. Mr. Hedwick has posted a guard at the stable now."

"No police?"

"No," Polly said. "He didn't want any publicity any more than I do… That's the story, Candid. That's all there is."

I chuckled and patted her cheek. "It's enough, lady. You've got the makings of a crime wave there…" I straightened and rubbed my chin. "You're prepared for shocks in this thing? Lister may be dead. It's quite likely he is."

"Oh, no!" she gasped. Then: "Are—are you serious, Candid?"

I shrugged. "He turned down ten grand. He saw the men who offered it to him. If they were serious, they want Bojangles out of the running on Saturday. They wouldn't stop at Lister's refusal. They'd put him aside and go to work on some one else."

She bit her mouth hard. "But why did they try to kill Lampoon then?"

I said: "Lampoon's the favorite in the Advance Guard, isn't he?"

"Yes. Bojangles is rated second best."

"That takes figuring," I said. "You give me a description of Johnny Lister and then you beat it home and stay there."

"All right," she said. "About five feet two inches. Sandy hair. Buck teeth. And he has a mole the size of a quarter on his left cheek. Blue eyes."

"Good," I said. "Take it easy, Polly. I'll be seeing you."

She got up and she came over and she kissed me. "I'll

do anything for this, Candid. I'll let you snap me in my undies in the fountain at Rockefeller Center if you say so."

I grinned. "That won't be necessary," I said. "Get out of here before you break my heart."

2

PLACE YOUR BETS!

ON THE PROWL again after four years. It was a funny feeling. Away from Broadway, cheap chiselers, crooks, killers, gamblers, con-boys, major and minor heisters, and going back just once to look them over!

Before I did anything, I telephoned the Morgue and asked for Big Tim Garth. Big Tim used to be one of the best on the force, but he hurt his left arm in a fall from a dock during a raid on a gang of warehouse riflers, and instead of retiring, he was allowed to handle the business of the Morgue.

When I got him, I said: "Hello, Tim. This is Candid Jones. Remember?"

"Glory be to heaven!" Tim Garth breathed. "And is it really you, m'boy?"

"In the flesh, Tim. How are you?"

"I can't be complainin'," he said, talking rapidly and thickly. "But it's you I'm thinkin' of at the moment. Glory be, there's been na hide na hair o' you in these parts since hell froze over. We heard yuh was takin' pictures of skirts and coats and hats for them women's fashion magazines. A fine business for as slick a gumshoe as ever nipped a dip!"

"Look, Tim," I said.

"Yeah, lad?"

"I'm expecting a stiff in there. It may be there now. Sandy hair, buck teeth, mole on the left cheek, small build—"

" 'Tain't here yet, Candid. We ain't got one like that around."

"If you see a mole—you let me know, eh, Tim?"

"I'll do that thing," Tim Garth said. "Are ye back in the racket, lad?"

"Just a one-shot," I said. "For a friend. You call me if you see a stiff like I said."

"A pleasure, lad." He hung up.

… After I called the Acme Agency and told them to forget about sending up the model, I took a shower and got dressed for the night.…

NOW WHEN I was sleuthing for the Apex Insurance Company, they used to say that I was hard-boiled. Maybe I was. I never was afraid of any man, and I always figured that if a guy was going to get rough with you, the best thing to do was to get rough with him first.

But you can't be hard-boiled without backing. I found that out. You can bluff so far and no further. Then you have to use the dukes. And then when the dukes give out, it's a nice thing to have artillery.

Sometimes, though, your artillery was taken away from you. I once had a single-shot derringer which I used in just such emergencies. I used to slip it in my sock garter in case I needed it. The plug-uglies never seemed to fan you that far down.

But I could do better than that now.

Before I put on a shirt, I strapped a Simplex Pockette camera under my right armpit in a home-made holster.

A Simplex Pockette is a small 16mm motion picture camera for amateurs. Only this one wasn't.

I'd stripped out the spring and the base for the fifty-foot film magazine, and I'd taken out the lens. Where the lens should've been, there was a .22 barrel. Where the spring should have been, there was a trigger. Where the film should have gone, there was a clip of nine .22 slugs.

The whole thing slipped under the arm like a tin of cigarettes. I had a plunger which operated the trigger run down the sleeve of my right arm and stop just under the cuff where it could be reached and depressed with ease.

A nice gadget. Life insurance, sort of.

After I'd put on my vest, I put on my shoulder holster—left side—and I unlocked my desk and took out my old Lüger. It was oiled and clean and loaded. I've always liked the Lüger. I've proven that it can outshoot a Colt or Smith & Wesson any day in the week, and it's overslung so that it balances like a scale in your hand. I jammed it in the holster cocked, safety on.

Then I hung my Leica Model G camera under my left arm so that it hung on my chest just under my coat where I could get it in a hurry if I saw something worth grabbing.

Business. Pleasure. Life insurance. I was set.

I went over to my studio window and glanced down into the street. There was no one on my side. But across the way in a doorway, two men were lounging, keeping an eye on my doorway.

Somebody was interested in me suddenly. I liked that. I put on my hat and coat and I went downstairs. I didn't pay any attention to the tailers. I caught a cab at Fifth Avenue and I said to the driver in a loud voice: "The White Slipper Club on West 45th, Mac."

"You've named it, Cap'n," the driver said, and we moved off....

Jimmy LaVerne owned the White Slipper, a small spindly man with a bald head, skirted by fringes of white hair over his ears. He had a deadpan. Only his eyes told the story. LaVerne was a white man. I mean, a square guy. Oh, the White Slipper was a gambling house with an innocuous night club front. Every one knew that.

But every one also knew that Jimmy LaVerne had never welshed in his life; his wheels were honest, his dice were honest, his cards were on the level. He was one of the few souls among the many heels of the main stem.

IT WAS JUST about nine-fifteen P.M. when I reached the club. I paid off the driver and went in. I left my coat at the hat-check counter and then went in to the bar. I had a lemon sour there, conscious of the fact that many of the boys were staring.

I said to the barkeep: "Where's Jimmy?"

"In his office," the barkeep said. He leaned forward. "Ain't—ain't you Candid Jones?"

"That's the name," I said.

I left the bar and I went back to Jimmy LaVerne's office in the rear. I saw quite a few of the boys around. I recognized a hood named Pinhead Riley. He jumped to his feet, startled, when he saw me. I avoided him and went into Jimmy's office without knocking, and I closed the door after me.

LaVerne was behind his desk, working on his books. He

hesitated a minute before looking up, and he said: "Yeah, friend? What can I do for you?"

"Lots of things," I said. "You're looking fit."

He raised his head slowly and gaped. It was the only time in my life I ever saw his deadpan break. He took the cigar out of his mouth and rolled his eyes. "For cat's sake," he said. "*Candid Jones!*"

"Sure," I said, taking a chair in front of him. "How are you?"

He looked at me a long moment.

"Fair," he said. Then his face snapped back into that expressionless mask it always was. "Heard you were doing pretty well with your cameras. Missed you around here. Been four years now. Sometimes—"

"Jimmy," I said, "who's got Johnny Lister?"

He stopped talking abruptly and took up his cigar. "I didn't know you were on the prowl," he said quietly.

"I am."

His eyes smiled. "That won't be liked by too many guys."

"My right's as good as it used to be," I smiled back at him.

"Glad to hear it. Is Johnny Lister the kid who rides Bojangles?"

I nodded.

"I didn't know he was missing," LaVerne said. "That's the truth. If I knew anything else, I couldn't tell you anyway. I keep my nose clean. Who you working for, Candid?"

"A friend," I said. "Tell me this then. How is the money going on the Advance Guard Handicap?"

LAVERNE STRETCHED AND settled back in his chair. "I'm glad to see you, Candid. Things have been a little too loose. Gives some guys the idea they're colossal shots. You get me. There's a smattering of money around. A little on Bojangles. Not much. I'd take that nag myself if the race weren't going to be crooked."

"What makes you think it is?"

"Too many cooks," LaVerne said.

"Guy named John Hedwick was in last night. He owns Lampoon. He was trying to find even money on his nag. Ten grand bet. Nobody took him. I'd have taken him at two to one. But not even money."

"Yeah?"

"Smart money's going on a nag named Lady Lou. I never heard of the goat before. Been plying the smalltown tracks, it seems. I don't think she has anything, but that's where the dough is going. At twenty to one."

"That makes you think there's going to be a crooked race?"

LaVerne nodded. "The smart money happens to be Alex Wolfe's. He's pushing around seventy-five grand that he's willing to bet at good odds. Most of it was taken by the suckers. There's a little left."

I asked: "Why don't you take it, Jimmy?"

LaVerne sighed and shook his head. "I'd like to, Candid. I'd really like to. But I know Alex Wolfe. You used to know him when he ran booze. He's a bookmaker now, a million-dollar bookmaker, so it goes. That means to me that Lady Lou wins the Advance Guard hands down, and hell and highwater can't stop that."

"Thanks for the info, Jimmy," I said. I got to my feet. "Have to leave you now… But I'll tell you something. You can skip the hell and highwater. Take some of Wolfe's money if you want to. I'll promise you that if Lady Lou wins the Advance Guard Handicap Saturday, she'll have to do it honestly."

LaVerne shrugged. "That's a big order for you, Candid."

"I know," I said. "But my friend happens to be the owner of Bojangles. And I'm not playing gumshoe for fun. See you around."

LaVerne got up and shook hands with me. "I always liked you, Candid. You're kind of conceited, but you never told me anything you didn't try to back up…" His eyes smiled again. "I'm going to take some of Alex Wolfe's dough. So long."

"So long," I said.

3

DOUBLE-TALK

I GOT MY hat and coat from the girl in the check room and I threw her a tip and put them on. Then I lighted a cigarette and I left the club and started over for Broadway.

I hadn't moved more than twenty feet when the two tails who had followed me from my studio fell in on each side of me and started to crowd me. "Take it easy," one of them said. "Keep walking."

I stopped walking and turned and had a look at them. The tall thin one I knew. His name was Doc Torrence. I didn't know the short one. He was young and simple-looking and his mouth jerked too much.

"Hello, Doc," I said. "It's been a long time."

"Now take it easy, Candid," Torrence said.

"Is this a stickup?" I asked, kidding.

"The boss wants to see you, that's all," Torrence said.

"Who're you working for, Doc?"

"Alex Wolfe."

"Come on," the young punk snarled. "Get going and can the chatter."

I stared at him and then I turned to Doc Torrence and I asked: "Who is this punk?"

"His name's Red Gilley," Torrence said nervously.

"I don't like him," I said. "He's young and fresh and I'm surprised at Alex Wolfe having a ginzo like this on his string. Outside of that, he's got a whiskey breath and he's kill-simple."

"Take it easy, Candid," Torrence cautioned.

"Why, you dirty flatfoot!" Gilley snarled. "I ought to blast you right here!"

"Skip that," Torrence told him. "Alex said for us to bring him in. How about it, Candid?"

"I'm busy right now," I said. "Tell Alex I'll see him at ten o'clock. And tell him all he has to do is telephone me. Tell him I don't like being herded by a pair of yellow punks."

The kid, Gilley, grabbed my coat and jerked me around. I let myself go with him. His eyes were blazing and his teeth were bared. Kill-simple wasn't the word. He had a .38 pistol in his right hand and he jabbed me hard with it in the ribs.

"The chief wants to see you *now!*" he snapped. "Get me?"

I looked at him a second and then I swung his gun away from me with my left hand and kicked him with the toe of my shoe in his right shin.

He yelped and started to reach for his leg.

That was when I lifted him off the sidewalk with a right from the sidewalk.

He fell on his back and he didn't move. I had his gun in my hand. I turned around and Doc Torrence was standing there with *his* gun out, shuffling nervously.

"Take it easy, Candid," he whispered, "take it easy now."

"Is that a gun, Doc?" I said. "Put it away. You know I don't like them and there's no sense kidding yourself. Alex Wolfe wants to see me alive…" I tossed him Gilley's heater. "You can give this back to him when he comes to."

Torrence put his gun away and slipped Gilley's in his pocket. Now listen, Candid—"

"You tell Alex I'll see him at ten o'clock," I said. "And if he doesn't like it, he can lump it."

I turned on my heel and walked down the block.

IT WAS JUST coincidence, my running into Polly Benefield ten minutes later. I was standing in front of the Times Building on Times Square when she came by.

She was with a good-looking guy, a six-footer with shoulders like a truck, and a smile that showed even white teeth.

"Candid!" she said when she saw me.

"Fancy meeting you here of all places," I said.

"I've been looking all over for you," she said, touching my arm. "This is Bob Gordon, my fiancé. This is Candid Jones, Bob."

"Glad to know you," Gordon smiled.

"The same," I said. "What is this about looking for me, Polly?"

"I tried to get you on the phone," Polly explained, "but you weren't at the studio. It's lucky we happened to run into you—"

"Why'd you want me?"

"Can we talk here?"

I shrugged. "As good a place as any. And I like being in the open with a wall behind me. Spill it."

She said quietly: "Johnny Lister is all right."

I glanced at Bob Gordon and then back at her and said: "He know about this thing?"

"Yes," said Polly. "Everything. He's been helping me—"

"Not much, I'm afraid," Gordon grinned. "I tried to find out—"

"Wait a second," I said. "I want you two kids to get something straight. If I play with this job, I play with it alone. I don't want either one of you sticking your noses into anything."

Polly stared at me and Gordon looked wry.

"I'm not being hard-boiled," I said. "Don't get me wrong. But I happen to know the boys who are on the other side of the fence. They play for keeps. Either one of you two find out something worthwhile and you're liable to wind up in the river with a milk-can over your skull. Now keep your hands clean and tend to your own knitting… Is that right?"

"Right," Gordon said.

"But I've got to tell you about Johnny," said Polly.

"Go ahead; You said he was all right."

"He telephoned me at six-thirty tonight," she went on. "He said he disappeared himself. He was afraid they might do something to him if he stayed around. He's all right. He's taken a room in a cheap hotel. He's going to stay there until Saturday morning."

"I get it," I said. "And then he'll arrive at the track safe and sound and all set to win the Advance Guard Handicap on Bojangles."

"That's right," Polly breathed. "I'm so relieved. I really thought something had happened to him."

"And you want me to quit this stint then, kid?" I asked, smiling.

"Well—" she said, "I'm sorry I—got so hot and bothered;

Candid, I'm such a fool—talking you into this and then Johnny being all right—"

"That's O.K.," I said. "You're forgiven."

"Oh, thanks, Candid. And you'll come out Saturday and see the race?" She was very earnest.

"Sure," I said. "On one condition. You let me know every time Johnny Lister calls you. Let me know how he is and what he says."

"All right," Polly said.

"By the way," I asked, "did he say where he was staying so that you could reach him?"

SHE SHOOK HER head. "No. He said he didn't want anyone to know. That would make him safer—if even *I* couldn't reach him."

"Sure, sure," I said. "Well—goodnight then, you kids. Have a good time."

"Good night," Gordon said, and Polly Benefield echoed him. Then they waved and moved off into the pedestrian traffic of Broadway. They were pretty much in love.

There wasn't any use hanging around there. I buttoned my coat and went into the Times Building and I went downstairs where the telephone booths were.

I took a booth and dropped in a nickel and called the morgue where I got Big Tim Garth again. "This is Candid, Tim," I said.

"Glory be!" Tim Garth said explosively. "And where in the name of Erin 've *you* been? A hell of a state o' things. Ye give me a description and ye ask me to let ye know and then when I buzz you ye ain't home."

"Business," I said. "Had to go out. What is it, Tim?"

" 'T is nothing," Tim Garth replied, "except that stiff

you was expectin' just arrived tonight. Sandy-hair with the mole on the cheek. Couldn't be any other."

"What happened?"

"Oh, the lad was shot twice in the chest. They found him floating past 22nd Street."

"East River?"

"Yes… Can ye identify him, Candid, lad?"

"I can," I said. "But I won't. Not tonight, anyhow. I'll be down to see you soon, Tim. I'll identify him then. And many thanks for the tip."

"Aw, go on with ye!" Tim Garth chuckled. "It's a pleasure, Candid. Any time I can tip you on any more of your stiff friends, let me know." He laughed dryly.

He hung up.

I hung up.

I thought, Well, that's that. Johnny Lister is alive—only he's dead. He's lying in the morgue but he telephoned Polly Benefield. He's stiff as beaverboard, but he's going to ride the Advance Guard Handicap. He's cold and calm on a smooth slab—but he's hot under the collar that some one may try to hurt.

"Double-talk," I muttered. "Clumsy damn thing to pull. Wouldn't fool a two year old. All the same—" I shrugged and went upstairs into the street. The clock on the Paramount Building read ten of ten.

I lighted a cigarette and walked down West 42nd Street to the old Apollo Theater, above which on the second floor, Alex Wolfe kept his mob and his offices.

4

PICTURES, C.O.D.

ALEX WOLFE WAS built like a hog. Only, it was as if the hog were standing up instead of being on all fours. His face wasn't so bad. It was round like the moon and his skin was dead white, as though it hadn't seen a ray of sun in years, and his jowls hung down under their own weight and gave him a tired aspect.

But his body was round and solid and stumpy and he was only five feet seven inches tall, and he looked overloaded, carrying two hundred and fifty pounds in that height.

He'd gotten balder since I'd last seen him. And he had two gold teeth in the front of his mouth now.

He stood behind his desk, the glare from the lamp on it reflected up in his face. He was grinning broadly. Against one wall, I saw Doc Torrence, smoking. Against the other, I made out a hood I'd known on the main stem four years before, Pinhead Riley—the same Pinhead whom I'd seen at the White Slipper earlier. I'd sent him up for a two-year rap once.

And close to me, watching me in a nasty way was the young kid, Red Gilley. There was hate in his eyes.

"Hello, Candid," Wolfe said suavely. "You haven't changed much."

"I haven't changed a bit, Alex," I said.

"Sure, sure. Have a chair."

I took the chair in front of his desk and propped it back against the wall in front of the desk. I like my back against a wall. I sat down. The place smelled of stale cigarette smoke.

"You got kinda rough with Red, I hear," Wolfe said, grinning.

"I meant to tell you about that," I said.

"Yeah?"

"You don't have to send me an escort, Alex. I figured you knew me better."

"Maybe *I've* changed," he said meaningly.

"Look," I said. "Come out in the open. I never did like double-talk. As for Red, he got rough first. All right, you wanted to see me."

"That's right," Wolfe said. "I wanted to set you right— what's that?"

I'd taken out my Leica as I talked and I pretended to toy with it. "That's a camera," I said, setting the lens at f/2., the focus at ten feet and the exposure at 1/10th of a second. "How about a picture?"

"No pictures of me!" Wolfe snapped.

"If you say so," I sighed, snapping him without sighting. I slipped the camera back under my coat.

"I don't like pictures," Wolfe said.

"All right," I said. "I didn't take any. What more do you want?"

He sat down. "Look, Candid. Let's get straight. Doc and Red here, I had them tailing the Benefield dame."

"Why?" I asked.

Wolfe laughed and glanced at Torrence. "He wants me to tell him," he said. "Ain't that nerve for you?"

"Keep talking, Alex."

"The Benefield dame sees you. And then you suddenly start prowling—"

"Prowling?" I said.

"Don't kid me," he said. "You haven't put your gams in the White Slipper Club since the night you quit the gumshoe racket. You're prowling. You've got a heater on you, I bet."

"Sure," I said. "It gets cold, these nights."

"Candid," Wolfe asked, "what did the Benefield dame want?"

"She wanted me to find a kid named Johnny Lister," I said. "You know why."

"No. Why?"

"You offered him ten grand to pull Bojangles Saturday. He refused. Then he disappeared. Polly Benefield thought something might've happened to him."

"You figured we'd bumped him off?" Wolfe queried. He laughed. "Ain't that hot? Listen, Candid, these aren't the old days. People don't get bumped off that way anymore. You're old-fashioned."

"My joints creak," I said.

"Hell," Doc Torrence said. "There's nothing wrong with Johnny Lister. I saw that kid downtown today. He was on 23rd Street and he was fine."

"That's funny," I said. "When I saw him he was on 22nd Street—in the East river—and mighty dead."

THERE WAS A silence. Nobody said a word. The gray smoke drifted up in stratus through the desk light. Then

Wolfe got up and walked over toward me slowly. "That's too bad. He was a good jockey. Maybe he should have played ball with those guys."

"Maybe," I said. "So now you know I know. And you won't have to waste nickels making phony telephone calls to Polly Benefield. I guess the idea was to make her think Lister was going to ride Bojangles, have her wait for Lister without another jockey, and then have her wait too long and fail to get her goat in the race. Kind of a childish plotto, Alex. Beneath you, sort of."

Wolfe stood in front of me and spread his legs apart. "All right, Candid, get this." He spoke very quietly. He was mad. He was trying not to look it, but he was rip-roaring mad. "Four years ago, you were a good dick. You were a hard-boiled bazooka and you had the boys tipping their hats to you. You also had an insurance company behind you. But times have changed."

"The New Deal," I said.

"You're soft. You're on your own. You haven't even got a private detective's license. And you don't bulldoze me a bit. I never was afraid of your big talk. I don't aim to start cringing now."

"Your boys feel the same way?" I asked.

"You're damn right we do!" Red Gilley said, choking on the words with his own vehemence.

"Well, Alex," I said as casually as I could, "I'll tell you. I think you're a rat. I think you're all rats. But these other ginzos don't know any better"—I smiled at Red Gilley—"you included. Alex, you're the biggest rat of them all. Because you're scared to death. You've always been scared to death. Not of me. Of the system you're playing—because no matter how you win, you know you're on the short end."

"He's gone in for uplift," Pinhead Riley remarked coldly. "I'm sick of this stuff, Alex."

"Me, too," Gilley snapped. "The sooner we bump this imitation flatfoot the better."

"I don't know," Alex Wolfe said, staring at me.

Things were tight. They were tight because Gilley hated me and didn't know any better than to pull his gun and start shooting. That was his only out and he had it on his mind, so I figured it was time to stop playing around.

I reached in my coat slowly and I pulled out my Lüger and I covered Alex Wolfe and looked at Gilley. "You never saw what a rod like this does to a man, Red," I said evenly. "It makes a hole in him. A real hole. Sometimes it makes two holes."

"For Pete's sake," I heard Doc Torrence breathe "it's that damned Lüger cannon again!"

"All right, Alex," I said. "All of you in the corner. I'm walking out of here tonight whole. No breaks. You know how I feel about killing. It doesn't bother me. So behave."

Wolfe motioned the others into a corner and backed up slowly himself, his hands limp at his sides. "Take it easy, Candid."

"I'm taking it easy."

"You weren't going to be bumped. That was just the kid spouting."

I laughed coldly. "You were afraid to take me."

Wolfe's eyes met mine with derisive calmness. "My last word, Candid. Keep your nose out and go back to photography. One more finger in this pie—talk to anyone about anything—and it's curtains."

"Look," I said, "I heard you were a million-dollar bookmaker. I think that's plain air. I figure you wouldn't be playing a long shot like this with your own money—not seventy-five grand worth. You're not that much of a gambler. Who's behind you?"

Wolfe's eyes got fishy. "Good night, Candid."

"Good night," I said. "Maybe you'll tell me his name Friday night. Suppose I drop in around eight."

"Suppose you do."

"It's a date," I said. "I'll have something to show you. A photo. It'll be one of my best jobs."

"Yeah?"

"Uh-huh," I said. "Picture of Johnny Lister a few seconds after he was shot in the chest. Don't follow me, gentlemen. I'm nervous tonight."

I left....

5

LAST RACE

FRIDAY MORNING, I went to the Morgue. I left the studio early because I didn't want one of Wolfe's men tailing me. I got down to the Morgue around seven-thirty.

I saw Big Tim Garth and I told him I wanted a picture of Johnny Lister's body.

"There ain't any sense in that," Tim said. "You can *have* his body. Take it off my hands."

"Not yet," I said. "Just a picture."

" 'Tis too dark in here," he said. "You can't take a picture in this light."

"Sure I can," I said. "This isn't a Brownie, Tim. Besides, I've got a photoflash. Is it okay?"

"Oh, blather," he said. "Take ye damn picture and be off with ye."

We went in and he took me to the wall and pulled out the niche whose slab held Johnny Lister's body. The stiff didn't look too good. Badly shot up and the river had been rough with it. I shot it with the Leica at f/11 letting the photoflash go after the lens was opened, then closing the shutter. There wasn't any worry about the subject moving. I shot the photo with the body in the lower half of the frame finder, which put it on the bottom half of the negative.

That was all I wanted there. I left and went uptown to the studio again.

I took the film cartridge out of the Leica and into my dark room. It was supersensitive film so I developed in total darkness. I underdeveloped it slightly because that would give me more latitude in printing.

When the negatives were dried from the blower, I spliced them in half, then inserted them in my auto-enlarger and went to work on the printing.

It was a mean job. It didn't work. I finally made a new negative from the two halves and when that was dry, I printed that.

You should have seen the photo.

It was as smart a bit of magic as I ever saw. I'd blown it up to eight by ten glossy so that every little detail stood out like a sore thumb. There, behind his desk, Alex Wolfe stood. He looked evil, because the desk light came up from below his face. A low light will always do that. He had been staring at me when I caught him. That made him look down. And in front of his desk—where I had spliced in the other negative—reposed the dead body of Johnny Lister. It was enough like a contact print to fool anybody.

I slipped the print into a manila envelope, backed by cardboard, and put it in my coat pocket.

It was one o'clock then.

I went to the window. Across the street in a doorway, I saw Doc Torrence and Red Gilley again. They must have been awful babes to figure they couldn't be seen there.

Oh, well. I called a cab and told it to wait for me at the front door. When it arrived, I went downstairs, hopped in, and rode off, leaving those two punks flatfooted in the doorway.

When I was sure they hadn't caught a cab to follow and after I'd had my driver make a few nifty turns to and fro, I said: "Fairview Park, buddy. And don't spare the horses."

Polly Benefield was in Bojangles' stall at the track with Bob Gordon, a guy named Shorty White, the nag's trainer, and a darky named Sam.

"Hello, Candid!" Polly cried when she saw me. "We've good news!"

"Yeah?"

"Bo ran the mile this morning in 1:49 flat! There's no other horse in this race can beat her time there!"

"What's this? What's this?" a new voice said. "Is Lampoon to be discarded so easily?"

WE ALL TURNED. The man in the doorway was smiling pleasantly. He was tall and thin and gray. His face was lined and there was a neat gray mustache on his upper lip. There were crow's feet around the edges of his eyes.

"Hello!" Polly said. "Spying on me! Candid—this is John Hedwick, owner of Lampoon. This is Candid Jones. Mr. Hedwick. I had him investigating Johnny Lister's sudden disappearance—"

"Oh, yes," Hedwick said. "But you said Johnny was all right, Polly."

"All right *now*," she said. "But I was worried about him then."

I looked at Hedwick and asked: "Any more attempts on Lampoon?"

"Oh, no, not a chance," Hedwick replied. "I've had a

guard around the stall. My trainer is all right. Bad bruise on his head, but he—"

I nodded. "Well, Polly, I've got some bad news for you."

"Y-you have?"

"Johnny Lister won't ride Bojangles tomorrow."

"But he will! He telephoned me this morning—"

"No," I said. "No. Johnny Lister didn't call you. Johnny Lister is dead. I saw him at the Morgue this morning. The boys who murdered him have been calling you. They were playing to have you wait for Lister to show up tomorrow. When he didn't show up, it would be too late for you to weigh in a new jockey."

Polly went white. Gordon held her.

"I say!" Hedwick snapped, looking stunned. He turned to Polly in quick resolution. "I've had enough of this beastly work. If it's true that Lister is dead—"

"It's true," I said.

"Then by Jove," Hedwick said with fire, "I suggest, Polly, that we call this thing off. We've lots of other races to finish our wager with. Lampoon and Bojangles needn't run in this particular one."

"That's fine," I said. "You're doing all right, Hedwick."

Hedwick's face dropped. "From your tone, you don't think so."

"Here's how it is," I said. "They want you to withdraw. Lampoon and Bojangles can beat any horse in this man's race. They can beat a horse named Lady Lou. But none of the other nags will beat Lady Lou. So if you two drop out, Lady Lou cinches it."

"I don't understand," Polly said.

"There's heavy money at big odds on Lady Lou tomorrow," I said. "Those playing the sugar want her to win—in a bad way, as you see."

"Oh."

"The best way you can show Johnny Lister what he'd have liked is to trim Lady Lou."

"I know, man," Hedwick said. "That's being very decent and sporting and all that. But I don't want my horse injured, nor do I want myself or associates placed in jeopardy."

"Nobody's going to be in jeopardy," I said. "I'm not on this for my health. And if there's fouling in the race, a protest and a little evidence will make it no race at all."

"That's enough for me," Polly cried. "I'll run Bojangles if it's the last thing I do."

"Well…" Hedwick sighed. "I can't let you outstrip me, Polly. Which means that Lampoon runs too."

After I left them, I scouted around the stables until I found Lady Lou's stall. I tried the doors of the stall but they were locked. Then a voice said: "Hello, Candid."

I turned around and saw Pinhead Riley standing beside me. "Hello, Pinhead," I said.

"The door's locked," he said.

"I found it out," I said. "Too bad. I'd like to have seen the nag. Are you following me?"

Riley shook his head and kept staring at me, his eyes expressionless and cold. "After what Alex told you last night, do you have to be followed?"

"Meaning?"

Riley shrugged. "He just said hands off, didn't he?"

"Now I wonder," I said, "who owns this horse?"

Riley smiled thinly and lighted a cigarette. "I do," he said.

I looked surprised. I couldn't help it. "Where did you—"

"Rich uncle," Riley jeered. "Left me five grand and instructions to buy a nag." I didn't smile, so he added: "You ought to put some money on her, gumshoe."

"I want to win," I said.

He came over very close to me and lifted his face up to mine and he said in a cold whisper: "Put some money on her. You heard me. It'll do you good. 'Cause if she doesn't win, you'll have seen your last race."

6

TWO WHO DIDN'T TALK

I STOPPED IN at police h.q. when I got back to town and I had a talk with Inspector Harry Rentano. You've heard of Rentano. He was with the Bomb and Forgery Squad for eleven years and he was the cop who broke up the Mafia single-handed. He was a little older now, but a fighting flatfoot if there ever was one.

"Hello, Candid," he said, grunting at me and then, grinning. "You're getting fat."

"You're not wasting away to a shadow," I said.

"No," he said, hitting his stomach. "*Tempis fugit* as the saying goes… I heard you were sleuthing again."

"Just looking around," I said. "I thought maybe you could take a few guys off my hands."

"I don't get you."

"Figured these guys might be wanted for something."

He chewed his mouth and shook his head. "We'd have 'em here if they were. Name me some names."

"Pinhead Riley."

"I'd like to have something on him.

"Doc Torrence."

"Clean."

"Could you want them for questioning?"

"Why?"

"I'm on something," I said, "that gets in Alex Wolfe's hair. He's been tailing me with a pair of his hoods. I want to lose 'em tonight. They stand in a doorway across the street from me."

"I'll pick them up," Inspector Rentano said. "What time?"

"About seven forty-five tonight."

"Sure, Candid."

"They know something about the Johnny Lister murder. You heard about it?"

"Big Tim called me. They do?" Rentano squinted at me. "Maybe I will question 'em at that. And where does Alex Wolfe come in?"

"I think he did it," I said. "I'm trying to prove it."

"Watch your neck, kid."

"Don't worry about me."

That night at seven-forty-five, I saw Rentano's prowl car pull up at the curb across the street from my place. Rentano got out and went over to the doorway with his gun drawn. I watched it with binoculars. Two men came out of the shadows. They were Doc Torrence and—was it Red Gilley?—no. It was Riley. Torrence and Riley. Gilley wasn't there.

They didn't argue with Inspector Rentano.

After the prowl car and Rentano and the two plug-uglies had gone off, I left the studio and took a cab over to the Apollo on West 42nd Street. When I got there, I paid off and then went straight upstairs to Alex Wolfe's offices.

They were there—Alex Wolfe and Red Gilley. Alex was sitting behind his desk, looking elephantine and ponderous, his eyes half-closed sleepily. He didn't even look at me when I opened the door.

But he didn't have to look at me because Red Gilley did. Gilley hated me. It was in his eyes and it was in his fist. When he saw me, he covered me with a .32 automatic and his gun hand trembled.

Alex glanced at Gilley and murmured: "Who is it?"

"It's Jones," Gilley said tightly.

"I thought you were clowning about that date, Candid," Alex said over his shoulder. "Well. Come in and close that door."

I closed the door. "I don't like that heater, Alex," I said.

"Put it away," Alex told Gilley.

"I'd like to cook him," Gilley said gratingly. "Of all the guys in the world, he's the one I'd like to take."

"When you grow up maybe," I said.

His eyes flickered and he put the gun away.

I CAME ALL the way in and moved around in front of the desk and Wolfe. Then I slowly took out the Lüger and held it carelessly off my left hip.

Wolfe looked at the gun in mild surprise. He asked: "What's the idea, Candid?"

"It's just here," I said, "because when I say what I've got to say, you guys may lose your heads."

"Don't be silly," Wolfe said.

But I could see that he knew no one had followed me—cops I mean—or else my gun wouldn't have been out for protection. And he licked his lips quietly.

"All right, Gilley," I said. "Keep your hands at your side and stand next to Alex."

Gilley said: "for two cents—"

"I know, I know," I said. "Get around."

He got around.

Wolfe smiled. "Well, Candid, it's your show. You've got a lot of splash here but I don't figure what it means."

"I didn't take your advice. I didn't keep my nose out."

"That's not news."

I shrugged. "O.K. then. Here's the business. Who killed Johnny Lister?"

Wolfe just smiled.

"Who's backing you, Alex?" I asked. "I think you'd better tell me. You can do a lot as state's evidence. You'd just cook as an accessory before or after the fact."

"You sound like my mouthpiece," Wolfe said. He yawned broadly. "Cut it out, Candid. This is horseplay. What'll you do—bump us if we don't talk and get strung for a kill yourself?"

"Not me," I said coldly. I reached into my pocket and pulled out the envelope and tossed it on his desk. He glanced at it. "Before you open it, get this. That's just a print. The negative is safe and sound and in the right place. You can rip that print if you want, but I can make a hundred from the negative."

Wolfe's expression began to change. He picked up the envelope slowly and took out the picture and stared at it. His eyes popped. Next to him, Gilley saw the photo and gasped in a hissing whistle.

"Pretty?" I asked.

Wolfe turned and looked at me. "You rat!" he said quietly.

"It's a hot job," I said.

"It's a frame," he said.

"It's an air-tight frame," I said, "unless you talk. Rentano wants you. And he wants your kill-simple morons. *I* want the guy behind you—the guy who's paying the sugar for these bets on Lady Lou—"

"I didn't kill Lister," Wolfe said. "This is a fake. It wouldn't stick."

"I'm a pretty good photographer," I said. "Rentano and h.q. would like to play ball with that photo. Rentano says he can get an indictment for first degree murder on it."

Wolfe watched my eyes, and my eyes didn't tell him a thing. His hand shook a little and he tried to smile but it was pretty sick. "Those cops—" He tried to get a breath. "They couldn't."

Gilley was tight as a drumhead. "The hell they couldn't. They can do anything they want! And with this dirty—"

"Never mind all that," I said. "What I want to know is, do you talk or not?"

"I didn't kill Lister," Wolfe said. None of my boys did either. We were all here the night—"

I shook my head. "No good, Alex. Maybe you're telling the truth. But if you were here and I took that photo here—"

"Jeez," Gilley said hoarsely, grimacing at me, red-eyed.

"It's the chair, Alex."

"No," Wolfe said. He waited a long time. "I'll talk." And he glanced over his shoulder at the door.

"Doc and Pinhead," I said, "won't be along. They're down at h.q. now, getting the hose from Rentano. It wouldn't do any good to bump me anyhow. Rentano has the negative."

WOLFE SMILED. "I thought maybe you'd slipped in four years. Oh well…" He looked at Gilley and shrugged. "I'll talk."

"Start."

"Doc and Red here were the guys who offered Johnny Lister ten G's to pull Bojangles." Alex sighed. "After Lister refused, the head man said Lister'd have to be wiped. Because he could identify Doc and Red, see? But I told the head man that wouldn't make no difference. They could just deny it. I didn't want murder in it, understand?"

"You're stalling, Alex."

"No, I ain't, Candid. This is on the level. The head man was nervous. He bumped Lister himself."

"I figured that," I said. "But you're stalling just the same. What I want to know is: who's the head man?"

Alex Wolfe opened his mouth to answer and there was a nasty savage crack at the same time. Wolfe jerked up suddenly and glared at me without seeing me, and then he settled back in his chair and seemed to relax, his eyes still open, his hands slipping off the desk.

I knew the sound and I knew Alex Wolfe was a quick corpse, and I heard the tinkle of an ejected cartridge on the floor and knew that the slug had come from a small-caliber pistol fired by some one on the other side of the door which had opened a notch.

But the big Lüger was in my nervous hand: and Red Gilley thought *I'd* shot Wolfe. He yipped in terror and went yellow with mingled rage and panic and reached for his own rod. He fired at me twice; both went wild, and his gun made a hell of a racket.

I didn't want to kill him. I wanted him alive. But I didn't like playing target. So I shot him in the left kneecap and he buckled and went down. It's a painful wound but he had it coming.

But when I got over to kick his rod away from his hand, I saw that he was dead too, and the hole in his head was too small to have been made with the Lüger. And besides, his knee-cap was smashed.

I went for the door—all this happened in about five seconds—and when I slammed the door open, there was another shot and a splinter from the door hit my cheek on the right side; and cut it, making it bleed.

The hall was like pitch. I couldn't see a thing. I fired a couple of shots into the dark for luck. I knew I hadn't hit anything. Then I jerked back and closed the door.

There were no more shots. The guy who had bushwhacked us had disappeared. I looked out the window to see if I could snag somebody coming out of the Apollo Building, but it was no good.

I called Inspector Rentano and told him what had happened. After he came, there was plenty of hell raised in that office. I didn't get home until two A.M.

7

CAMERA!

THE SUN WAS shining; the weather was warm; the track was fast. I got out to Fairview Park around twelve noon. The place was jammed. I marveled at the crowd.

At half-past, I went over to the paddock where I'd arranged to meet him, and found Harry Rentano in plain clothes, smoking a little brown cigarette-size cigar. He was enjoying himself.

"Hello, Candid," he said. "I hope you ain't going back on your word. But even if you do, I'm having a good time. I haven't been to the races since I—"

"Since you were a good detective, I know," I said. He grinned.

"Well," he replied, "how good are you? You promised me a killer today. If you think I'm going to have a picnic with three hot murders on my hands, you're crazy."

"Did you release Riley and Doc Torrence?"

"Didn't have to," Rentano said. "They called a lawyer and were sprung. *Habeas corpus.* They got out this morning after I got back. Around four A.M."

"You put tails on them?"

"Uh-huh," he nodded. "Casey and Lane. Calling h.q. every half hour."

"All right," I said. "Pinhead Riley is your man."

"You mean—?"

"No. He's your man. Find him and hang onto him. Don't let him out of your sight from now until the Advance Guard Handicap is over."

"I get it," Rentano nodded. "But I want to call h.q. first."

We went down by the grandstand and underneath it where the telephone booths were. And Rentano called his office. When he came out of the booth, he looked a little pallid and he'd thrown his cigar away. "I'd like to know what the hell is going on," he said nervously.

"What's happened?"

"That was Casey."

"But I thought he was tagging—"

"He was tagging Doc Torrence, yeah. But Doc Torrence is with him now. Dead. Same slugs as got Wolfe and Gilley last night and Lister in the bargain."

".25 caliber?"

"That's it. Now listen, bright boy. Who is it and why? I can play so far, Candid, but I've got responsibility and you haven't. It's my neck. You've got nothing to lose."

I smiled. "Only my life."

"Is it Riley?"

"I don't know," I said. "Cover him."

I lost Rentano in the crowd and I went up to Bojangles' stall. It was one o'clock then and the races had started. I could tell from the sporadic cheering of the grandstands.

Polly Benefield, looking very pretty even if worried, was up in the stall with Bob Gordon. "Candid," she said, "is everything going to be all right?"

"If that horse is any good," I said, "you've won a race

already. Things are O.K., kid. You and Bob here have a good time and root for your nag. Got your new jockey engaged all right?"

She had. The jockey was a little colored lad named Tiny Duke. He was the son of Sam, the trainer's helper. I took the kid aside and I said: "Now look, Tiny Duke. Bo's got to win this race."

He grinned. "She gwine to, suh."

"Fine. But do me a favor. Keep down on her back, way down."

"Do what he says," Sam told his progeny.

"Yassuh," Tiny Duke said. "Ah lay low."

I LEFT THERE and went up toward Lampoon's stall and that was where I met Inspector Rentano and Pinhead Riley. I saw suddenly that Rentano had the nippers on Riley and the other end of them was around Rentano's own wrist.

"What's this?"

"Oh," Rentano said carelessly, "I caught this doodle fooling around Hedwick's stall, so I figured I'd better harness myself to him to make sure of things. Now he can't go nowhere without me, and he can't talk to no one without me. He—my friend—is on the ice."

"Well, that makes it nice," I said.

"It does?"

"Yeah. Both Lampoon and Bojangles are in the running. That makes it tough. Now the guy whose behind all this has laid almost a hundred grand of sugar on this race, betting on a goat named Lady Lou. He kept himself in the background by working through Alex Wolfe. I know Wolfe knew who it was. I don't think any of the others—including Riley—knew the identity. He bought this horse for Pinhead Riley through Alex Wolfe. Riley is just a figure-head to own the horse and maybe slip it a speed-ball. Wolfe was to handle the betting and collect. But the head man was in the background, covering, doing the necessary kill-ing, taking the long shot chances."

Rentano looked grim. "What happens now?"

"Now," I said, "the head man is in a jam. All horses are running. And Lady Lou probably isn't getting her speed ball which puts her out of the running against nags like Lampoon and Bojangles. So the head man can do one thing."

"What?"

"Murder a horse or a jockey and have the whole race called off. That saves his money."

A bugle blew out on the track. Riley stirred uneasily. "That's it, smart guys," he growled. "Let's see it anyhow."

"Run along," I said, and I left them and went up to Lampoon's stall. They were leading. Lampoon out toward the paddock. He was a nice-looking piece of horse. I saw John Hedwick watching him with a smooth Graflex camera in his hand. He was taking some pictures. I went to him and said hello.

"Why, hello, Jones," he said.

"Everything all right?" I asked.

"All right in my stall. Is Polly—?"

"Things are set," I said. "There won't be any trouble. The police have nabbed Lady Lou's owner. He was going to speed up his nag with a shot of hop. But no go. This race'll run honest or not at all."

"Jove, that's good news. Takes a weight off my mind. Are

you going down to the rail with Polly? I'd like to watch with you all, if you don't mind."

"Come on along."

Hedwick gave some last minute instructions to his jockey and then we went through the crowd to the rail where we found Polly and Gordon. They both had cameras out, a Kodak and an Ikomat and they were shooting the parade past the post when we arrived.

"What is this?" I asked, "Photographers' convention?" And we all laughed.

I swung out my Leica and joined them, along with Hedwick's Graflex.

Suddenly there was a roar that started low and soared up to a shrieking maniacal crescendo: *"They're off!"* Some one pushed in beside me. It was Rentano with Pinhead Riley. Both tense, their eyes on the fleeing nags. I looked at Polly Benefield and Gordon. They'd gone mad. They were purple with shrieking. Hedwick gripped the rail. His knuckles went white against his skin as he shouted hoarsely. The trainers chimed in then. It was an ear-wracking all-pervading din.

We were situated almost opposite the barrier. As soon as the horses had broke, they were away from us and down beyond the grandstand into the second quarter.

I couldn't see anything. I didn't know who was leading. I couldn't hear the amplifier above the tumult of that crazy mob. I finally saw the horses when they reached the three-quarter post across the track. They looked like jerking peanuts. The din was terrific. You couldn't have heard the Alcazar go up in that blast of noise.

THEN THE NAGS came into the home stretch. Polly stopped screaming and took a picture with her camera.

"*Jove!*" Hedwick cried. "Lampoon's leading! She's going to win! I must get a picture of that!"

He held the big Graflex close to his body and peered down into the ground-glass finder, flexing himself to take the photo while the crowd went hysterical.

I came next to Hedwick quickly and I jabbed the Lüger's black mouth against his left side hard, on a line with his heart.

I said: "No picture, Hedwick."

He didn't take it. He stared at me a second, then down at the Lüger which is not a pretty picture at close range. His mustache worked jerkily. "I—I say—"

"No pictures," I said. "This race is going to finish."

"By Jove!" he cried. "I don't understand!"

"No," I said, "*I* don't understand. I don't understand why a Graflex takes a picture with the operator's hand stuck in the back through a false felt cover. I don't understand how a Graflex could take a picture without a film pack or a lens. Cut it out, Hedwick. This is the end of the line. You get off here."

"But—"

"You've got a .25 caliber pistol in that camera, the muzzle where the lens should be. A good gag, Hedwick. I use it myself. You were going to plug Bojangles or her jockey when they came into the stretch."

"But I assure you—"

"Then your jockey was to pull Lampoon and let the long shot, Lady Lou, skid by to win. You're the ginzo who bumped Lister and backed Alex Wolfe and turned him off when he started to talk. You figured the roar of the crowd would kill the sound of a small caliber shot, muffled by the Graflex."

Hedwick said slowly, "A long shot in itself."

"A long shot all around," I said. By then the nags had romped home and Polly Benefield was screaming happily that Bojangles had taken the race, and she was kissing Bob Gordon and he was waving his arms. "Hear that? The play is over. That's the curtain line."

"Oh, well," Hedwick said, "it was a good gamble." He turned toward me slightly, looking very tired and old, and without warning I felt a stab in my left side and then I heard the muzzle blast of his gun and I knew he'd fired at me from the Graflex.

There was too much of a crowd as he moved away. He fired another shot. I couldn't take a chance at him with all those people behind him. When his second slug missed me, I jumped his gun and kicked the Graflex out of his hands, catching it over my toe like a pig skin. It fell on the ground and smashed and the .25 heater—a compact little blue-steel Colt job, neat but not gaudy—came out of the debris.

Hedwick dove for the Colt in a last chance and I lifted him off the ground with my foot in his chest as he stooped over and then I fell on top of him and swung the barrel of the Lüger against his jaw with everything I had. He went out, of course, and there was a rotten sound as the jawbone snapped.

He felt stiffer than a ramrod underneath me.

I got to my feet and ripped off my coat to take a look at my wound. It was under my left arm, a four-inch gutter that looked bloody and terrible and stung like the devil—but wasn't serious at all.

Everybody was staring at me, and at Hedwick out cold on the ground, and at the two rods. Rentano jerked Pinhead Riley over and yelled: "For gosh sake, Candid, what in hell—?"

"There's your killer!" I cut him off, mad because I'd been a fool to get shot at like that. "What do you want me to do, tie him up in Christmas wrappings?"

NEAT BUT NOT GAUDY

*Candid Jones Learns That When an Ex-
Dick's Ex-Wife Is Framed for Exterminating
an Ex-Lover, You Can Expect Excitement*

1

OVER MY DEAD BODY!

IT WAS ABOUT eleven o'clock in the morning, and I was busy photographing a pair of legs in stockings for an ad for the Sheer-Shine Hosiery Company, when the door of my studio opened and Inspector Harry Rentano, chief of homicide in New York, walked in, carrying a tabloid.

"Hello, Candid," he said, waving.

"Hello, Harry," I said. "Have a chair and pour yourself a drink. I'll be finished in a couple seconds."

He sat down just as I fixed my lights. He whistled. I couldn't blame him. His wife, Kate, was a swell dame, but she didn't have the neatest gams in the modeling racket like Claire Crosman. When the photofloods were set, I took a look and knew I had it right. I made six exposures.

Rentano was smiling. "No wonder you like this racket. There's more in it than meets the eye. Listen, Candid, do they really pay you for the pleasure of taking pictures like that?"

"They pay him," Claire Crosman smiled, "and he pays me for letting him take them."

I looked at Rentano and shook my head. "The way you talk, you'd think you hadn't seen a pair of legs before. You—with four kids."

Rentano flushed. I turned to Claire and said: "That washes this up." And I paid her off. "Ten o'clock Tuesday for the cigarette account. Sport clothes."

"I'll be here," she said. And she left.

I went over and put my plates in the dark room and then I came back and sat down next to Rentano and asked: "How're things with you, Inspector?"

"They're okay with me," Rentano said. But his face fell, and sober lines began to run through it, and he avoided my eyes as he took out a tin of miniature cigars and lighted one. "But they're not so hot with you."

"I can't complain," I said.

"Not yet you can't," he said. "But you don't know. I take it you haven't seen the morning papers yet, Candid?"

"No."

He studied me deliberately and I waited, beginning to feel annoyed, because I didn't like this beating about the bush. At last he said: "I never knew you were married."

The thin man let go two noisy
bullets which hit Lazarus

I said: "I'm not."

"But you were."

"Yeah?"

"You married Gladys Merwin in 1930," he said. "And she divorced you in 1932. She went to Reno and her complaint was incompatibility."

"That's right," I said. "And frankly, I don't see that it's anybody's business but my own, and I don't see that—"

"Candid," Rentano said softly, "it's everybody's business now. It's public. And it's got everything to do with my coming here. I don't like to give it to you this way because for all I know you may still be in love with her—but—" he tossed me the tabloid—"have a look."

I stared hard at him a second, and then I picked the paper out of my lap and I looked at it. It was the Post-News, a morning rag that took great delight in crucifying people who didn't have a chance anyhow. The managing editor was a ginzo named Fred Lucio and he hated my face because I once punched him hard for a piece of libel. That

By that time, I was on the floor, rolling like the devil

made it a criminal libel rap and he'd have served time if the rag hadn't settled out of court.

Half the front page was a headline.

Sleuth's Ex-Wife Slays Lover!

The other half had a picture of Gladys Merwin, a picture of the corpse, and a picture of me, taken back in 1932 when I was gumshoe for the Apex Insurance Company. It was a rotten picture.

"Never mind the rest of it," Rentano said. "The guy who wrote it used his imagination. I'll give you the straight stuff."

I LOOKED AT him, feeling a little cold and numb. "She didn't do it, Harry."

"I knew you'd say that," Rentano said. "But you'd better hear it first. If the district attorney knew I was up here shooting off my mouth—"

"He wouldn't like it," I said. "It's white of you, Harry. I appreciate it."

"Oh, hell," Rentano said, shrugging. "You always played ball with me, Candid. Outside of that, you got me out of a nice spot last month when you snagged Hedwick on that Bojangles racehorse thing… But I want to ask some questions first."

I said, "You're not casing me?"

"Don't get me wrong. Candid. I want a better picture of the setup, that's all."

"Go ahead then."

He leaned back. "Tell me how you met Gladys Merwin and how you married her."

I took a breath and remembered. "She was twenty-two then," I said. "Pretty as hell. She was playing the ingénue lead in a music-comedy, *Red Horse Tavern,* at the Forest Theater. I saw her and I fell for her. I gave her a rush. It was one of those things. We eloped to Elkton, Maryland, in a week."

"Why didn't it last?"

"We didn't hit the ball. She liked parties and people. I didn't. Then she made a picture in Hollywood. She was away for half a year. That didn't do any good. Then she wired me that she'd fallen for a guy named Gordon Lazarus—some actor out there—and she said she wanted a divorce. I was fed up myself. I told her okay."

"And she divorced you?"

"In Reno. Just a wild kid, Harry. She liked a change of scene, couldn't stay with one guy too long. But she was aces."

Rentano shook his head. "Did she marry Gordon Lazarus?"

"Yes, I think she did."

"Where is he now?"

"I don't know," I said. "In Hollywood, maybe."

"Well, Candid," Rentano said seriously, looking kind of sad about it, "your ex-wife is in a first-class jam. She'll be indicted by a grand jury next week. I happen to know that the D.A. is out to get her. It'll be a quick trial and an early trial. And between you and me and the *Post-News,* she's going to be convicted of first-degree murder and she's going to die in the chair."

I said, "You're covering a lot of ground, Harry."

"I know, I know," Rentano sighed. "But I can tell,

Candid. I've been a cop too long. You know my record. I've been around." Which was true. Rentano was an ace, had been around plenty, Bomb and Forgery Squad, broke up the Mafia, put the big-time rackets on the skids, wiped out the prohibition Heniker mob. "Last night, Candid, about two A.M., I got a call from the manager of the Hotel Montafloras on West Fifty-fourth Street. I went right up there with a couple of the boys. I found your ex in her own rooms on the tenth floor. She was hysterical, crying and screaming. She kept saying, 'He's dead! Oh he's dead!' The stiff was a guy named William Rickert. He was on the floor with four slugs in him. Two in the head, two in the chest. Not a miss anywhere. I found the gun on the floor. A .32 Colt pistol. Four shots fired from it… There you are."

"The Colt did the shooting?" I asked.

"So the micrometer says."

"And who was this William Rickert?"

RENTANO SHRUGGED. "THAT'S what makes it tough. I don't think your ex can beat the rap because of this Rickert guy. He was an inventor, Candid, something in the electric refrigerator line, and worth plenty of dough. And he was a married man—with one kid… Nice people. He lived on West Fifty-seventh Street."

"Yes?"

"Gladys Merwin said that he'd been chasing after her, making love to her, but that she had been repulsing him, knowing about his family. But the setup at the district attorney's office is that they had been going on like that and he suddenly got remorseful and wanted to give her up, and she shot him. That's hard to beat. You know it is. Jealous mistress angle is always bad because it pulls no respect with a jury. And no jury is going to believe their friendship was platonic."

"It's all circumstantial," I said. "But it's good stuff. It'll convict her."

"Yeah?"

"But why don't you think she killed him, Inspector?"

Rentano looked startled. "Hey! I didn't say—"

"Cut it out," I said. "There's no green in my eyes, Harry. I've been around too. I know damn well you wouldn't waste time coming up here and spilling all this to me if your conscience didn't hurt. You don't think she did it. You want to see her get a chance for her life. And you figured that Candid Jones, ex-sleuth and ex-husband, might be the guy to turn the trick."

"You called it," Rentano admitted reluctantly. "And here's the flaw as I see it. Gladys Merwin was as hysterical a case as I ever arrested. I had to take her to St. Luke's hospital for treatment before I put her in the can. You get what I mean?"

"I get you."

"Yet," he went on slowly, his words sounding ponderous and profound, "that Colt pistol didn't have a fingerprint on it."

I stared at him without saying anything.

"You see?" he said. "It's the only point in her favor—a slim one, but a point. Would a hysterical woman—after she had shot and killed a man—think coolly about wiping off a pistol and then putting it down on the floor where the cops could find it, heh?"

I said no.

Rentano put out his miniature cigar and exhaled a long

blue finger of smoke. "That's got it then. I just thought you might want to do something about it."

Rentano put on his black hat and moved toward the door. "Drop in at headquarters some time and chew the fat with me," he said nonchalantly. But he stopped at the door and turned. He looked short and plump there, and there was something intense in his swarthy round face. He would have made a swell picture then. He was every inch a smart cop, and yet a family man, a guy with a sweet wife and a knockout kid daughter. I could see it as he stood there and I knew what that intensity meant even before he said, "I'm sorry as hell, Candid. If I could do anything, I would, but I'm official and my hands are tied. I didn't mean to give you one over the heart. There was the chance you were still in love with her. I didn't like that."

"No," I said, smiling slowly. "Not that, Harry. But she's still a square kid."

"That's even better then," Rentano said, more cheerfully, "She'll get a square deal then."

I replied, "If she sits in the chair, Harry, it'll be over my dead body."

Rentano watched my eyes and he saw that I meant it and he didn't smile. "I know. Good luck, kiddo. If I can do anything, let me know."

He went out.

2

EATING CROW

IT WAS GETTING to be a habit. But what could I do about it? I'd had my tummyful of the gumshoe racket when I quit it in 1932. That had been four years before. I'd sleuthed for the Apex Insurance Company as their trouble-shooter, opening up phonies on their policies, but mostly recovering hot ice. I'd had a lot of luck and I'd had the breaks and I'd built up a rep.

They used to call me Candid Jones in those days. Not because I was crazy about candid cameras (which I was) but because I was younger then and I didn't like to waste words. I said what I thought and I backed what I thought with my dukes—and sometimes with my Lüger. It got around the main stem and the underworld that I was tough. Well, maybe I was hard-boiled. But I had to be. That was my front. With a front like that, I could get things done.

I quit Apex in 1932 to let a hobby of mine become a business. Cameras and photography. I'd been daffy about them since I was a kid. I went into the business—commercial photography—and I made out. I built up a good clientele in those four intervening years—and I made money.

Then Polly Benefield, a swell little society dame whose mater I once helped recover some rocks, stepped into the picture. After four years, she came to me to go back. She was in a jam, a nice kid, somebody trying to kill her horse, Bojangles. Maybe you remember that one. I went back. "Just this once," I said to myself. "Just this once...."

But it wasn't once. It was twice. For here I was again, getting into harness. If I'd helped a kid break clean, it stood to reason I couldn't let Gladys Merwin fry for a killing that wasn't hers.

It seemed natural getting the armor on once more. Under my right armpit went the Simplex Pockette, strapped there. The Simplex Pockette is a small 16mm motion picture camera, magazine-loading. But this one was a little different. In the first place, it had no lens. Instead, there was a barrel where the lens should have been. In the second place, it had no motor. There was a clip of .22 caliber bullets where the motor should have been. In the third place, it had no film. There was a trigger where the film should have gone.

It made—on the whole—a nice article in the event of a last gasp.

Then I slipped on the big Lüger in its cowhide holster. Left shoulder.

And then a camera. I'd been in the habit of wearing a Leica G whenever I went out. There was no telling what a guy could pick up in the way of pictures with a fast lens like that under his coat. But it always attracted attention. And I'd just put together something which wouldn't.

Using an ordinary wooden-sided cigarette case with a built-in automatic lighter with a hole in one end of the case where you ignited simply by puffing on the cigarette, I took out everything inside and where the hole was, I installed an f/1.5 lens. It was a special job and it cost two hundred iron men. It had a universal focus. Then by putting two spools in the case and winding a strip of 8mm film on them, I had enough raw film for twenty-five exposures. A small knurled knob on the side automatically wound up on the film as each snap was shot. In this way, I could pretend to take it out to have a cigarette and get a picture surreptitiously. A nice gadget.

I took a cab downtown because I wanted to see my ex-wife and talk to her. She was in the Tombs.

The guy at the desk was a lieutenant. A little triangular name-plate on the desk said he was Soho McLean.

"I want to see Gladys Merwin."

McLean stared hard at me. He was a big man with a broad mouth and his eyes were cold as glass, and dead gray on top of it. And he had muscles in his jaw, developed from sticking it out. So I knew he wasn't too soft.

"Have you got a permit for that rod?" he asked coldly.

I said I had.

"Let's see the permit," he said, "and let's see the rod."

IT WAS EASY to spot the Lüger. You can't carry a pistol that size under your coat and look like an Esquire ad. You've got to bulge a little.

"Oh, for cat's sake," I said, annoyed, "I've got a permit. I've had a permit for this gun since Hoover was elected. My name's Jones. Terrence—"

"I know who you are," McLean snapped. "Candid Jones. You made a big noise as a shamus a couple of years ago, but that don't carry no weight here. Hand over."

I gave him the Lüger and I showed him my permit. He took his good time before he gave them back. I said dryly: "Thanks. That makes the Sullivan Law still sacred, doesn't it?"

"Yeah," McLean said slowly. "But you can't see the dame."

"Why not?"

"I don't answer questions, buddy," he said, chiseling his face into something marble. "Scram."

"I want to talk to her," I said. "I used to be married to her. I'm not her attorney."

"Listen," McLean said. "If you were smart, you'd know she's being held forty-eight hours incommunicado. That's inside the law. And that's the way it is. And there's no bail so's she'll stay in the can from now on. I feel kind of sorry for you, in a way. Must be kind of tough to have the papers splashing your name all over the front page along with the floozy." And he half-smiled.

I got a little hot. It was the way he said it, and the nasty little smirk at the end. I walked over and leaned down on the desk close to his face and I said evenly: "You're a pretty tough guy in uniform. I didn't know they had bigheaded punks like you left on the force. But I'll tell you something. That crack costs you a wallop. You'll get it when you're off-duty, the day Gladys Merwin is released. And you'll get it across your dirty mouth." I turned on my heel and started out.

"That's very interesting," McLean jeered from the desk. "Don't run away, Jones. I won't hurt you."

I said: "I'll be right back, flatfoot, to watch you squirm."

Down the block I found a drugstore and I went in and found a telephone booth and called the homicide bureau where I got Inspector Rentano.

"Hello, Harry," I said, "Candid."

"Yeah, Candid?"

"I just tried to see my ex. I've got to get her story, Harry, if I'm going to do anything."

"I know, I know, What's the matter?"

"I had a run-in with a cop named McLean."

"Soho McLean?" Rentano whistled and then he chuckled. "That guy—they say he eats flat-irons for breakfast, Candid."

"He'll eat crow," I said, "one day soon. He's got a nasty mouth."

"Didn't think much of Gladys, eh? Don't be too hard on him, Candid. Soho is mid-Victorian. He's got a thirteen-year-old daughter who's nuts to go on the stage. He's scared to death she will."

"What's that got to do with the price of eggs?"

"Don't you see? Soho McLean thinks all show girls are from Satan himself. He sees a potential extortionist, blackmailer or con-woman when you say the words 'show girl.' It's like a bull seeing red."

"Show girls are good girls," I said "I never knew a better bunch than Gladys' friends at the time we hitched."

"Cut it out," Rentano said. "You sound like a preacher. Okay, Candid. I'll buzz the district attorney and tell him you want to comfort your frau and he'll put the Indian sign on McLean. Wait about ten minutes and then go back."

"Thanks, Harry," I said and hung up.

I waited ten minutes, smoking a cigarette, and then I went back.

McLean was still at his desk, but his lips were pressed together and he looked a little pale.

"Well, flatfoot," I said, "may I see Miss Merwin *now?*"

And McLean squirmed.

3

THE LADY CAN'T REMEMBER

SHE WAS LYING on her cot when the Screw left me in her cell, and she was crying very quietly. I could tell that because her shoulders were shivering slightly. She didn't look up when the cell-door opened and grated shut. She just didn't seem to care.

They had her in prison gray but even the drab dress couldn't take away from her looks. She'd always been a knockout because she'd never grown up. People who think young seem to stay young. Her dark hair was a little wispy, and I could see that she didn't have any make-up on. For all of that she still could have packed them in.

I said: "Hello, Snooks."

She stopped the shivering of her shoulders and she slowly looked up. There were four gleaming lines down her cheeks where her tears had run. And she saw me and smiled slowly. "Oh, darling," she whispered, biting her mouth, "you're homelier than ever. Your beautiful red hair is the same—but those freckles and that nose—it's got longer—"

"Take it easy, kiddo," I said.

She shivered and closed her eyes. "Why—why did you come, Candid?"

"To get you out of this hole," I said.

"No...." Her voice was hollow. "You can't get me out, darling. Nobody can."

"You didn't do it. I can get you out."

Her head fell into her hands. "Ah... it's so easy to say. Get you out, get you out. But—" she shook her head slowly—"it's not that easy to do. I've been thinking and thinking all night long, ever since they put me here. It's been—oh, horrible, all of it!" She looked up suddenly and stared hard at me. "You said I didn't do it. You believe that. I can tell by your eyes. And you never did lie. I love you for that, Candid."

"Sure," I said, smiling wryly, "but that doesn't put anybody on first base. So suppose we start putting the picture together."

"You'll have to ask the questions," she said. "I don't know where I am at this point."

"Sure," I said. "Hold it a second." I got up and went to the bars and I looked at the Screw who was standing outside, just out of vision, and I said: "On your way, big ear. And tell Soho to stop imitating a moving picture cop."

The Screw flushed, startled at being caught, and he moved away. I went back to Gladys.

"Talk in a whisper," I said "I'm sitting next to you on the cot. Take it slow and easy and keep it quiet. Now tell me what happened when Willie Rickert died last night."

Gladys' eyes shot wide in the horror of recollection. "But I don't *know* what happened last night," she said hoarsely.

"You mean you were drunk?"

"No, no, not that. I mean—well—Willie Rickert had called for me after the evening performance—"

"I didn't know you were playing," I said. "What show?"

"*Top Flight!*" she said, "Toni Schulberg did the piece. We opened two weeks ago. It was a flop. I think Schulberg was keeping it going on nerve, to try and salvage a little of the money put into it, but it's losing ground fast and it shouldn't have lasted a week."

"Go ahead."

"WILLIE RICKERT CALLED for me at my dressing room after last night's performance, and then we went to the '44' Club on West Fifty-second Street and we had supper and danced. Willie was nervous and he kept saying that he had to tell me something."

"Yeah?"

"Finally we left the '44' and took a cab for my place. I have two rooms at the Montaflores, you see? Well, on the way—in the cab—Willie turned to me suddenly and he kissed me as though it were for the last time and he said: 'Glad, I've something to tell you. You may hate me for it.' I got a little frightened. I asked him what it was. And he said: 'I'm a married man, Glad, and I have a boy. I'm sorry I didn't tell you about it before. But it's off my chest now.'" She caught her breath hard, remembering. There was real pain in her eyes.

"Wait a second," I said. "This is on the queer. You didn't tell Rentano that story. You told Rentano that Rickert had been chasing you and that you'd been avoiding him because you didn't want to be mixed up with a married man—"

"What else could I say?" she asked plaintively. "Wasn't it bad enough the way they found me? I couldn't tell them the truth. They'd never have believed it! I had to tell Rentano that story—it came right to me when he asked me—it was the first thing I could think of—"

"Then," I said, "you'd been living with Rickert?"

"Yes." There was a long dead pause. "I loved him, Candid. It was different somehow. Not like you and I. Not like Gordie Lazarus either. It was the first time I ever really loved anyone I think."

"And you didn't know he was married?"

"Not until last night when he told me in the cab."

"What did you do?"

"I—asked him what we were going to do. He said he wanted to marry me, that he was going to get a divorce from his wife. He said he'd told me first, that he was going to tell his wife about me the same night. I asked him why it had come to a head. 'Because,' he said, 'I've been afraid. Some one has been blackmailing me, making a muck out of the fact that I'm in love with you, threatening to tell Edith'—she was his wife, I guess—'about our meetings. I've been paying through the nose with fear but no more. I'm coming out in the open now. The hell with the scandal. If you want me, we'll go through it.'"

I asked: "Did he mention who the backmailer was?"

Gladys shook her head. "No. He didn't say. Well—we reached the Montaflores and we went up to my rooms. I told him to pour himself a drink and I went into my room by myself and I was upset and I wanted to be alone a few moments. All of a sudden—" a tremor shook her body—"the shots—the four shots, cracking like—" she gasped for breath.

"Easy does it," I said.

"—I rushed in and Willie was on the floor and he was

dead. I knew it the instant I saw him. I screamed. I must have blown my top, Candid. Everything else is a blank until I left the hospital with Mr. Rentano."

"You didn't see the gun?"

"I don't remember it at all."

"Rentano said you were hysterical," I said. "You blew your top all right. But didn't you hear voices, a door opening, anything that might—"

"I didn't hear anything but the shots," she said.

"You're a big help," I said, smiling.

The corners of Gladys Merwin's mouth got very white. "I'm no help at all. I know it. I didn't kill Willie Rickert, but that won't stop me from dying. Perhaps you'd best keep out of it, Candid. There's no glory in a lost cause."

"Cut it out. You talk like an actress. Now give me this: who knew you and Willie Rickert were carrying the torch in no uncertain fashion?"

"Nobody knew except the two of us," Gladys replied, "at least—far as I know—I'm sure Toni Schulberg suspected. Yes, Toni must have known…. But Fred Lucio couldn't have known."

"*Lucio!*" I snapped. "Where does that rat come in this scenery?"

SHE LOOKED SURPRISED. "Oh—that's right! He's editor of the *Post-News* and you once had a fight with him. I was out with him the night I met Willie Rickert. The new opening of the French Casino. Lucio introduced me to Willie. That's the last time I saw Lucio. He tried to paw me that night and I told him to head in."

"Look," I said, "how about Gordon Lazarus. Didn't he know? What's he been doing all this time? Where—"

"Of course!" she exclaimed.

"Keep it low."

"Gordie Lazarus knew. That's why I wrote him to come on to New York. I wanted to divorce him. We've been separated for nearly a year. The agreement was that when one or the other wanted a divorce, it would be okay. I wrote Gordie last month."

"And he's in New York now?"

"Yes. He's at the Warwick."

"Things get better," I said "Anyone else? Think now. Did anyone see you—"

She snapped her fingers. "Wade Lamont!"

Wade Lamont was a bright-eyed boy who pulled down two grand a week. His daily column was syndicated in one hundred and thirty newspapers from here to Honolulu. He had peeped through more keyholes, covered more news beats, broken more hearts, and caused more disaster than a peeping Tom, Daffy Dill, John Barrymore and the Johnstown flood, respectively. He worked for the *Post-News* and was the only reason anybody ever bothered to read the rag.

I asked: "What about Wade?"

"He must have known! He saw Willie Rickert kissing me one night at the Kit Kat Club. We were just going in and Wade was coming out when Willie, a little tight, kissed me."

"Button the lip and understand me," I said. "I'm on my way now but here's what you do. Keep quiet, don't sign anything, be a sphinx. You go up before the Grand Jury next week. Maybe I'll have you out of here then. Maybe not. Your lawyer will be Abe Herschell. I'll engage him. Sit tight."

"All right, Candid."

"And while you're sitting tight, I want you to remember. Willie Rickert could have been killed by the guy who was blackmailing him, the blackmailer being afraid that Rickert would see the D.A. and spill, especially after Rickert told you he was going to confess to his wife about his clandestine association with you."

"I wondered if maybe that—"

"Maybe, maybe," I said. "But it doesn't hit me. Because the blackmailer could have killed Rickert neatly and in numerous places. This way, it was worked out so that Rickert's death left a first-degree murder rap right in your lap."

"You mean," Gladys said slowly, "the one who killed Rickert wanted me to die, too, under a legal pretext?"

"Kiddo," I said, rising, "you get a base on balls. Take it easy. Don't let 'em scare you. I'll see you."

And I went out with the Screw.

4

WHEN HUSBANDS MEET

I PICKED UP a copy of the bulldog edition of the *Post-News* at Broadway and City Hall and then I took the Interborough uptown. I was ashamed to be seen with the rag, even in a subway.

But I was interested in what Wade Lamont might have to say about the Rickert-Merwin thing.

His column was called MANHATTAN AND HOLLYWOOD and it consisted mostly of two syllables words because Wade Lamont didn't know how to spell them over that. He was thick enough to be sensational at times, and he had pipe-lines in every major studio on the West Coast, and every night club on the East Coast. If you liked the lowdown—dirt or otherwise—he had it, and his column held the circulation of the paper.

So I opened up the sheet and found Lamont's stint and I read it. And I hadn't gone very far before I found out something that Harry Rentano hadn't told me.

In the middle of the column, Wade Lamont had written: "Talk about having a nose for news!.... Your correspondent was the first scribe on the scene last night when Gladys *(Top Flight)* Merwin shot and killed Willie Rickert, refrigerator tycoon, at the Montaflores. I'd seen Gordon Lazarus earlier in the day, who flew in from Hollywood recently to sue La Merwin for divorce in this state. I was on my way up to see what La Merwin thought of it. Need I remind you that infidelity is the only ground for divorce here?… Another queer angle of the killing. *Top Flight,* the Toni Schulberg musical at the Apollo, which was starring La Merwin, will not open tonight, there being no understudy. And maybe Schulberg isn't glad! Ask Toni about La Merwin's contract…. Candid Jones, Gladys Merwin's first hubby, lends the yarn a nice twist. Four years ago, he was sleuth for the Apex Company and the most hardboiled dick on Broadway. But he retired in '32 to make impressions on gelatin. Ironic, eh? Not that he could do anything about the case now…."

I threw the paper under my seat. That wasn't going to do Gladys any good at all….

At the Warwick Hotel, I didn't bother to ring Gordon Lazarus before I went up. I just found out his floor and room number and then I stepped in the elevator.

I knocked at his door. I stood there a full minute before he answered it with a wary: "Who is it?" And his voice scratched as though he were scared.

I said: "Police. Open up."

Another short wait. Then the door opened timidly. I spread my hand against it, pushed it back, and stepped into the room. He closed the door. I took a look around. Just a regular room, but a nice one. Small desk, bed, bath, two windows. I sat down close to the windows.

Lazarus walked over toward me, staring at me half-curiously,, half afraid. He was a pretty-boy, black hair slicked on his skull, no chin, prickly mustache, and flashy clothes.

You know—an actor trying to look as though he'd arrived when he really hadn't had his option taken up.

"Take a load off your feet," I said "I want to talk."

"You're not a cop!" he cried, recoiling suddenly.

"No," I said, "I didn't think you'd open up. So I said that."

"I wouldn't have opened up," he said, still standing. "And you can take it on the lam right now. I'm not talking to any newspapermen. I've had enough of that stuff."

"Sure," I said. "Sit down."

It was really funny. He was scared and he was trying to act tough, but I could see that he'd have died if the bluff didn't work. He was damned nervous, his fingers scratching his palms red, and his mouth working so hard, it twitched as if he had St. Vitus dance.

"Are you going to get out? Or do I have to call the—"

"I'm not a newspaperman either," I said. "Now sit down and talk. We've got a lot in common. My name is Jones. Terrence Jones. They call me Candid. I was married to Gladys before you were."

HE WENT ABSOLUTELY white and shivered. He breathed: "Candid Jones!" in a voice like a bent saw. He fell into the chair opposite me and kept watching me, gripping the arms of the chair.

"Well? Well?"

"What do think of what's happened?" I asked.

"I had nothing to do with it," he said nervously. "I don't know anything about it."

I cocked an eyebrow. "I didn't say you had. I asked you what you thought. But now that you mention it—why the hell are you so jittery about it?"

"I'm not jittery! I don't know anything, I tell you!"

"Yes, you do," I snapped, getting sore. "So let's skip the double-talk and get to the point. You knew about Gladys and this Rickert stiff. You knew all about it. She wrote and told you about it. She wanted to marry Rickert. She asked you for a divorce. She even paid your fare to New York so's she could talk it over with you. I'm telling it, ain't I?"

"That's right," Lazarus said, relieved. "Sure, she wrote and I came. That's the truth."

"She wanted a divorce."

"That's what she said."

"That's what she said all right," I said coldly. "But that doesn't explain why you told Wade Lamont that you'd come East to divorce her for infidelity, does it?"

Lazarus started breathing hard. "Now wait a second, Jones. Don't get me wrong on this—"

"You told Lamont that last night," I said. "What changed your story?"

"I didn't tell Lamont that! Maybe he just made it up on his own!"

I got up and grabbed his shirt front and pulled him out of the chair. "What changed your story, Lazarus? Who paid you to change the story?"

"For goodness sake—!" he cried, blanching.

"I'll draw pictures for you," I said. "You came East to talk over a divorce with Gladys. But you got ideas. You knew Rickert was a married man, a father. Gladys didn't. You started putting the touch on Rickert, bleeding him by threatening to spill to his wife and maybe the papers. Finally Rickert got tired of paying. He said he was through. You got panicky, you figured to bump him—"

"No! No!"

"—bump him," I went on, "and fry Gladys for the job. Maybe you have a nice policy on her life—"

He hit me on the jaw and tried to push me away. It wasn't much of a blow. I let go of him and let him have the back of my right hand across his face. It knocked him down. I stood off and waited for him to come up again for more.

He came up but not close to me. He backed off against a wall.

"I'll tell you something," I said. "You didn't kill Rickert. You haven't got the nerve for a neat job like that. You're yellow."

"I told you I didn't do it," he said.

"Then why'd you change your story? Why'd you tell Lamont a thing like that? You didn't think that kind of stuff would prove Gladys guilty in the eyes of a jury, did you? A hell of a chance she has to beat the rap when her own husband takes a powder on her! Do you know what you've done?"

"I didn't mean to do a thing like that," Lazarus said. "I was just scared. I didn't want to get mixed up in it."

"You've branded your wife just what the D.A. is going to try and prove to a jury—a dizzy showgirl who was taking a married man for a sleigh ride."

"They—they won't convict her," Lazarus mumbled.

I LOOKED AT him steadily and there was ice in my eyes. "They'd better not convict her. If they do—let me give you a tip, Lazarus. I may have been born in Galliopolis, Idaho, but I've been around the city a long time."

"I don't get you, Candid."

"It's this. An accessory after or before the fact is just as guilty as the murderer. Does that sink in? I mean, if a guy from Hollywood happened to *know* who opened Gladys' door last night, plugged Rickert four times, then tossed the heater into the room, clean of prints—"

"I told you—"

"—if a guy just happened to know who it was," I cut him off, "and didn't tell the cops but maybe tried to blackmail the killer, squeeze him for a little dough, and if the cops finally did catch up with the killer then—" I took a deep breath, "—then a guy might fry along with the killer."

Lazarus didn't say anything but his lips moved.

"Think it over," I said.

"Maybe," Lazarus faltered, "—maybe I ought to—"

The door behind him opened quietly and quickly. Two men stepped in. They closed the door behind them. They were both tall men, one thin, one fat. They wore snapbrims, way down over their right eyes. The thin one had a long face and he wore glasses that were too big for his nose. The fat one had a pan that was all jaw and no nose. What had been a nose was mashed against his face.

"Stickup!" said the fat man calmly.

"Take it easy."

He had a Colt .38 automatic in his hand with a long tubular silencer fitted by thread to the end of the barrel.

The thin man had a blue-steel .32 revolver in his right hand. It also had a silencer threaded over the end of the barrel.

I said: "Look, mister. Didn't your mother ever tell you the facts of life? A silencer won't muffle a revolver."

"Muffle it enough," said the thin man with the glasses. He smiled toothily. "You Lazarus?"

"No," I said. "He is." I flicked my thumb toward Lazarus, who had moved around the other side of the room, facing them, his face very pallid.

The fat man stared at him. "You Lazarus?"

I was watching the muzzles of those rods and figuring what the chances were of jumping them when Lazarus, finally getting a good look at the plug-uglies, gasped—as though in recognition and then cried, as though in pain: "Jones—for goodness sake—this is no stickup! These guys—"

He never got a chance to finish. The fat man squinted his eyes, there was a quick *plop* sound, and I knew that Lazarus had taken a slug from the Colt pistol. I saw Lazarus knocked forward, and I knew too that the slug had caught him in the stomach and that he was through.

The fat man tried another as Lazarus fell, but the silencer had killed the ejection by recoil of the first empty cartridge and the pistol jammed.

By that time—three or four seconds in all—the Lüger was out and I was on the floor, rolling like hell for the protection of the bed and I fired at the boys twice without even seeing them and noticed the long thin splinter of wood which the revolver cut out of the bottom of the bed, trying for me.

I went under the bed and spun around for another shot, but I only had time to throw a pellet at a rubber heel vanishing through the door as the gunmen faded fast.

I went after them. They made the staircase and disappeared down it. I followed. It was a long chase down those stairs from the sixth floor and I knew before we reached the lobby that I'd lost them.

I put my Lüger back in its holster, feeling kind of good because I had had enough time to use my cigarette-case-camera on the rapid-fire action upstairs.

Three things were certain. Gordon Lazarus was dead. Gordon Lazarus had seen the guy who bumped Willie Rickert. Gladys Merwin was innocent.

I took the subway downtown to the *Post-News*.

5

NEWS AT THE *POST-NEWS*

"NOW, WAIT A second, Candid," Fred Lucio said, getting up and raising his hands defensively.

"Hello, rat," I said. "How's the crucifixion business going?"

"Now take it easy, Candid," he said. "This is a scandal sheet and you know it. It's run that way. If the boss says smear your ex-wife on the front page, I've got to smear her. You know I don't like you, and I know you don't go for me. But lay off me. It isn't my fault. This is just my job."

We were standing in the city room of the *Post-News*, and things were pretty busy. The typewriters were clacking, and the boys of the Fourth Estate were running around looking harassed, and a couple of them had stopped and were staring at Lucio and myself.

I said: "Sit down before you faint, Fred. Even your own pencil-pushers are interested."

Lucio looked at the guys who were staring and bellowed at them to take it on the lam. Then he sat down.

"They've got memories," I said. "The last time I came in here, they saw me wallop your chin."

"Lay off!" Lucio snapped. "Maybe I had it coming to me, but it's *fini*. What's on your mind, Candid? If it's the Rickert case, I can't do a thing. Sue if you want or take another sock, but it's out of my hands, I tell you."

"Look," I said. "Maybe you've got a decent streak in you somewheres at that."

"Never mind the sarcasm."

"I want to know a couple of things," I said. "And you're supplying the answers."

"Oh, nuts," he said. "Skip the double-talk. You always came to the point in the old days."

"That was because I knew where I stood," I said. "I'm not so sure on this one. Where were you last night at two A.M.?"

Lucio smiled thinly. "Ah! I get it now! On the gumshoe trail again to clear the ex's fair name, heh? Stick to your pictures, Candid. She's as guilty as all hell."

"Uh-uh," I said. "I know better. This morning I only thought she wasn't guilty. This afternoon I know it. For instance, take a guy like you: you knew she and Rickert were carrying on. And you knew Rickert was married and had a kid. And you had made a play for Gladys and been struck out. Follow me, Fred? It gets more interesting as we go along. Suppose you need a little dough. You put the bite on Rickert, blackmail him so that you won't tell Edith, his wife, he's galavanting with a showgirl. He pays. Then he gets tired paying. He threatens to expose you. You bump him. Sore at Gladys, you bump him prettily so that the rap lands in her lap—"

"Goshamighty!" Lucio breathed. "I'm glad you're not a cop!"

"But I am, in a way," I said.

"But she did it, Candid! Hell, I don't know anything

about it except I introduced him to her. Sure, I made a play for Gladys. I struck out. I've been struck out before. You don't put murder on a dame's head because—"

"I know. Besides the police have arrested her. She'll be tried. She'll be convicted."

"After all—look, Candid. I don't need dough. I'm fixed. I wouldn't squeeze a guy—and especially Rickert! I went to college with the guy!"

I said: "You're in a hell of a dither. I take it you haven't got an alibi for last night."

"As a matter of fact—"

"Okay, skip it." I watched him hard. "Do you read all of Wade Lamont's garbage before it's printed?"

Lucio nodded, frowning. "Sure."

"Why'd you clip a squib he wrote about Willie Rickert kissing Gladys in front of the Kit Kat Club recently?"

"He didn't write such a squib."

"You sure?"

"Ask him yourself. He's in. He just got in."

"Thanks, Fred," I said. "I'll do that. But keep your own nose clean. And don't get too rough with your scareheads or you and your boss will both wind up on your backs."

"I'm scared to death," he said, looking annoyed.

WADE LAMONT'S OFFICE was close by Lucio's desk in the city room. I went in without knocking. The room was a wreck. A couple of typewriters with copy paper strewn all over the place and a dictaphone sat in front of his desk.

Lamont was behind his desk, gray fedora back on his graying hair, cigarette cocked in one corner of his broad mouth, his hands clasped behind his neck. He was talking to his secretary when I came in, dictating his next-day's blast. He stopped when he saw me and he looked startled. He said laconically: "Hey!"

"Hello, Wade," I said.

"Candid Jones!" he said. Then to his girl: "Scram, Ruth, maybe this guy has the lead for the column. Have a seat, Candid. What's on your mind?"

"You," I said.

"Gunning for me with the old cannon?" he said. He roared laughing. "Yeah, I heard! I was down at the Tombs to get the lowdown on your ex-femme. I heard you had a run-in with Soho McLean." He laughed again. "Imagine the flatfoot asking to see your permit—*you!* You mustn't mind Soho, Candid. He belongs to the Gay Nineties and doesn't know it yet. Ain't he got a honey of a name? Reminds me of Ed Wynn. You know—soooo!" He laughed again.

"Never mind the act," I said.

"I heard you were sleuthing again," Lamont said. "If I can help you out—"

"Remember the night you bumped into Gladys kissing Willie Rickert at the Kit Kat Club?"

His eyes narrowed. "Yeah. I remember."

"Lucio says you didn't write a squib on it."

"So what?"

"Why didn't you?"

"I don't figure that's any of your business."

"I figure it is," I said. "Especially since a guy was blackmailing Rickert because of the connection. For instance, you could have held the squib out, then squeezed him for dough. If you'd printed it, his wife would have seen it and there wouldn't have been any chance for a squeeze."

"You're slipping," Lamont said. "When a guy pulls down two grand a week, he don't blackmail."

"There's something in that," I said. "That's what bothers me. Why did you kill the item?"

Lamont pulled down his mouth and thought it over. "Oh, well," he said finally, "what the hell. Off the record, Candid?"

"Off the record," I said.

"Edith Rickert—Willie's wife—happens to be a swell dame. The kind of dame you don't find but once in a blue moon. Understand me? I knew about Willie and Gladys long before that night at the Kit Kat. But I kept it out of my column because I didn't want to see Edith dragged into a lot of mud."

"That's damned big for you," I said. "You and your drivel. There's a catch somewhere."

"I'm telling you, Candid."

"You sound like you've got a crush on Edith Rickert."

Wade Lamont pulled his hat over his head and leaned forward. "Maybe I have," he said coldly. "But that's my affair, see?"

"No," I said, "I don't see quite. But maybe I'll get the point after a while." I got up.

"Hell with you," Lamont said.

I went out....

6

ACTION COMING UP!

I FOUND A telephone booth on the corner of Barclay Street and I dropped a nickel in the slot and called the homicide bureau. Inspector Harry Rentano answered.

"Hello, Harry. This is Candid."

"I gathered as much," Rentano sighed. "A day of complete hell and you have to ask questions."

"It's about that rod," I said. "The one on the floor of Gladys' room when you found Rickert. Have you traced it yet?"

"We traced it," Rentano said. "That part was easy. We traced it to the Apollo Theater. And it sews up the case, Candid. Your wife hasn't got a chance now. May as well know it. I'm sorry as hell, but that's the way it is."

"I don't get you," I said.

"Look," Rentano explained, "in the second act of *Top Flight*—that's the play your wife was in—there's a shooting scene. For the property, they had this pistol. The property man missed it last night after the show was over. He thought he'd misplaced it and he kept his mouth shut because he didn't want to lose his job."

I said: "But this A.M. when he read the papers, he figured

Gladys Merwin had hoisted it from him and had used it on Willie Rickert, so he came forward and gave his story."

"Not exactly. He said he told Toni Schulberg, the producer, and she told him to tell the police."

"Who *is* this Toni Schulberg, anyhow?" I asked.

"Damn if *I* know. I've been trying to reach her. But they haven't seen her at the theater all day. And she's not in her own apartment. And nobody's seen her. The last place she was seen was the '44' Club last night. And she was with Gordon Lazarus, your ex-femme's hubby. What a mess!"

"But if she hasn't been located, how did the property man tell her the gun was missing from his equipment?"

"He told her at the '44' Club right after he found it out. We've got him at h.q. here. And he's got a good story. As soon as the pistol was thought missing, he went to Toni Schulberg in the '44' and he told her the story. He said that she looked at Lazarus and cried: 'You heard that, Gordon? The pistol's gone! We've got to find Gladys and Mr. Rickert immediately!' And then she jumped up and she and Lazarus left the spot."

"Why do you want her, Harry?"

"Because—dammit—Gordon Lazarus is dead. Shot and killed at the Warwick this afternoon! And Candid, if you know anything about it and don't spill to me, I'll put the Indian sign on you for life."

I laughed. "Harry, remember your wife and kids! You wouldn't want a stroke."

"Be serious."

"All right. I know something. I'll tell it to you later. And here's a funny one. I've been figuring all this time that Toni Schulberg was a man. And now I find she's a dame. Which changes things considerably… Sit tight, Harry. I think I'll have Gladys out of the can tonight. And you can tell Soho McLean he's due for that wallop sooner than I thought."

"When can you give, Candid?"

"A little while," I said. "First a spot of dinner and then maybe a fracas. No evidence yet, but I'm not going to need it. You stick by that phone, Harry. I think this case has broken."

"I'll stick. Make it snappy." We both hung up.

7

SOUP

I STOPPED OFF in a stationery store and bought a little box and wrapping paper. I took out my camera-cigarette case and I put it in the box. Then I wrote on a card: "Harry: this is a camera. Unload and develop film in total darkness. The two yeggs are the guys who gunned Gordon Lazarus. Find out who's behind them and you've got the guy who killed Rickert." I signed my name. Then I wrapped the box up, addressed it to Harry Rentano, put on some stamps.

"I wonder if you'd do me a favor," I asked the saleslady, a loyal spinster if there ever was one. "I wonder if you'd hold this package for me. If I don't call for it by tomorrow noon, would you drop it in a letter box for me?"

"We'd be glad to," she said, and she took it.

"Thanks," I said, and I left.

It was dark then, in the last stages of a deep purple twilight. Those kind are cheap in autumn, but cheap or not it was a honey. The street lights had just come on. It was just past the rush hour and traffic was getting lighter. I hailed a taxi cab and got in and told the driver: " '44' Club on West Fifty-second and make it snappy."

The driver put the car in first, and stepped on the gas, and as we moved away from the curb with the crate roaring noisily in low gear, something cracked the window behind my head and a splinter of glass stung my neck.

There wasn't any sound other than that, no blatant shot. Yet, when I turned and wiped a drop of blood from my neck, there was a slug hole in the rear window of the cab, not more than four inches from the spot where the back of my head had been in sight.

The driver of the hack didn't even know anything had happened.

I tried to have a look out back, but we were moving. It was darkish, there were other cars, people on the sidewalks; I didn't see a thing that would help.

So I didn't say anything. And I slumped way down in the cab out of sight and I stayed there until we reached the '44' Club at seven P.M.

The '44' Club was a cross between El Morocco and Sherman Billingsley's Stork Club. It took a nice crowd, elite and theatrical main stem, and there were usually no hams or muggs because Clyde Simmons—who operated the spot—wouldn't stand for any rough stuff.

Clyde Simmons was a nice guy. He'd been an actor once and then a producer. Finally, when show business began to go on the rocks with pictures up and doing, he quit the stage and opened up the '44' with a new idea: a good dinner and a swanky two-hour floor show: all for the price of the meal.

I hadn't even ordered my dinner when Clyde came over and sat down with me. He spoke very quietly. "Glad to see you, Candid. It's been a long time. But right now isn't the spot for amenities. You're hot."

"Am I, Clyde?" I asked.

"You're red-hot," Clyde Simmons said in a low guarded voice. "It's been whispered. It's reached me. Somebody's got a finger on you."

"I know," I said.

"I've got a message for you," he said. "Toni wouldn't trust anyone but me. She called me before noon. I'd been hoping to see you."

"Toni Schulberg?"

"She's laying low," Simmons said. "She has her reasons. I suppose. She wants to see you."

"What for?"

"About Gladys Merwin."

"Do you know anything?"

"That's all she said."

"Where is she?" I said.

"She said she was at your studio," Simmons said.

The waiter left a Martini and I picked it up and drank it slowly and turned, to get a glimpse of the door. "Look, Clyde," I said. "You're facing the door. The tall thin guy with the cheaters there. Dark blue suit."

"Shep Coxe," Simmons said without raising his eyes from the table. "Bad case, Candid."

"Kill-simple?"

"That's the tag. He just came in. Right after you."

"Oh," I said, "he's mighty interested in me! He's been following me all day long, especially since he missed me with his slugs when he and a tall fat ginzo washed up Lazarus."

SIMMONS PALED AND wet his lips. "I hope to God you know what you're doing, Candid. The fat boy is Phony Shapiro. They do a brother act for a fee. Their last job I know of was bodyguarding Fred Lucio of the *Post-News*. He wrote an editorial against bookmaking at municipal racetracks. His life wasn't worth much for a couple of days until he retracted."

"Let's have a phone, Clyde."

Simmons called a waiter and the waiter went off and brought back a handset which he plugged into the booth where I was sitting. I called headquarters and got Harry Rentano again.

"I'm ready to give, Harry," I said.

"And about time," Rentano exploded. "Kate's called me twice in the last ten minutes and handed me the old nick. Supper's waiting and me not home yet."

"My watch says seven-ten," I said. "Is yours with it?"

"Yeah."

"At seven-thirty I want you to raid my studio. There may be shooting. I'll be there. Toni Schulberg will be there. And the twin guys who killed Gordon Lazarus will be there. Their names are Shep Coxe and Phony Shapiro."

Rentano said calmly: "I've heard of them. Is this the pay-off, Candid?"

"This is it."

"Seven-thirty. I'll be there."

I gave the phone back to Clyde Simmons and I said: "I want a big favor, Clyde."

"Ask it," he said.

"Shep Coxe is herding me," I said. "I'm hot all right. But I don't figure whether he aims to try for me outside or wait until I get home. I don't want to take any chances. It's got to happen after I get home."

"Well?"

"I want a waiter to hold him up. There's a fin in it for the waiter."

"Just a second." Simmons called a passing waiter. "Enrique!"

The waiter came over. "Yes, sir?"

"This gentleman wants you to do something. There's five fish for you. Do what he says."

Enrique grinned. "For a bonus, anything, sir."

"Go back to the kitchen," I said, "and come out with a tray loaded with soup. When you pass the man who's sitting in the first booth to the left of the doorway—see him—?"

"With the glasses?"

"—that's the guy—then you trip and spill the soup on him."

Enrique laughed. "What is this—a rib?"

"That's it," I said. "A rib." And when he left, I said to Clyde Simmons: "Put this order on the cuff. There won't be any time for paying now."

"Right, Candid."

"Here he comes," I said.

Enrique came out of the kitchen holding a tray above his shoulder. He had soup all right and lots of it. It was steaming there. He passed my booth. I got up and followed right behind him. Shep Coxe saw me coming and he started to get up when Enrique lammed into him and the soup went everywhere. I heard Coxe yell in fury and pain for a second and I think he cracked one to Enrique's chest, but I got outside fast, into a cab, and snapped my studio address on West Forty-fifth Street.

We went off in a cloud of dust...

8

TOO MANY CLUES

I PAID THE driver before we reached the studio. I didn't want to be standing in the street for long. When he pulled up at the curb, I went out on the run and into the doorway. I had my Lüger out then just to make sure. I went upstairs carefully, but I didn't see anything of the other gunman, Phony Shapiro.

I unlocked my door and went in.

The lights were on, of course. Toni Schulberg was sitting in my big leather armchair which has a bottom that keeps falling out and makes the cushion soft as silk. She looked as though she'd been dozing and when she heard me she came out of it like a terror and leaped to her feet, her pretty eyes wide in horror as they focused on the maw of the Lüger.

I closed the door behind me. "Easy does it, lady," I said. "I'm Candid Jones."

She still stood, looking frozen.

"I am," I said. "Clyde Simmons sent me."

She sighed and fell into the chair and for a second I thought she'd passed out. But no. She was just feeling relieved because she groaned: "Thank goodness!" And she stared at me and added: "I never saw you before in my life,

Candid, but I was never so glad to see anyone else in my life either."

I put the Lüger away and gave her a look-see. She was a good-looking woman, brunette, about twenty-nine or thirty.

She had a nice round small mouth and dark eyes and she was dressed in a wine velveteen outfit and a gray coat with a light fur collar. She looked all right. I thought it was too bad she had to have a terrific moniker like hers.

"When I saw that gun—" she said, rolling her eyes.

"I know how you feel," I said. "I've had some slugs pass me by today."

"You—? But why—?"

"I was with Lazarus when he died. I saw the boys who got him. Shep Coxe. Phony Shapiro."

"Yes," Toni murmured. "They would have done it. *He* couldn't have taken the chance then… That's why I came here. The second I heard they'd got Gordon Lazarus—"

"I'll tell you why you came here," I said. "You and Gordon Lazarus saw who killed Willie Rickert last night."

She shook her head. "Not exactly. But we saw enough. I didn't have what the police could call evidence. So I couldn't go to them for protection. But Clyde said you were a right guy. Here I am."

"For protection?"

"That's it," Toni smiled. "I'm too young to die." She leaned toward me. "And you don't want Gladys framed on a rap that isn't hers."

"Then let's get down to business fast," I said.

"All right," she said.

"I'm going to tell you," I said. "You saw who took the property pistol from the *Top Flight* backstage last night."

"Yes—at least—I saw him by the property table."

"You forgot about it. You went to the '44' with Gordon Lazarus. When your property man found you there and told you, Gladys Merwin and Willie Rickert had left. You immediately guessed that Rickert was due for a slug."

"Yes."

"Why?"

"Because Willie had been blackmailed by the man who killed him."

I took a deep breath. "Wade Lamont, you mean."

She gasped. "Yes—Wade! But how could you know so soon?"

"I'll tell you," I said. "I figured this way. Rickert didn't make an outcry. Which means he never saw Lamont and never saw the rod that killed him. Which, in turn, means that Lamont fired through the crack after opening Gladys's door just enough to snake his hand in."

"Go ahead," Toni said breathlessly.

"RICKERT WAS SHOT while sitting on the sofa to the right of the door. A right-handed man would have had to open the door wide to get his gun hand around the edge of the door. But a left-handed man would have had it easy. He'd have been sighting from the left, and he wouldn't have had to open the door as far. That way, Rickert wouldn't have seen the gun."

Toni was very pale. "Is Wade Lamont—"

"—Left handed? You bet he is. I saw him this afternoon. He was smoking. He had a clip of matches on his desk beside him. The matches in the clip had been torn off *from the left side!*"

"Go on."

"You and Lazarus went after Gladys and Rickert. Tell me what happened when you reached the hotel."

"We got out of the elevator," Toni said, "and we walked down the hall to Gladys's rooms, which were around the corner of the hall. Just as we reached the turn, we bumped into Wade Lamont. He gasped in terror when he saw us and he shook like a leaf. 'Get out of here!' he cried. 'She's just killed Rickert! Don't get mixed up in it!'"

"What did you do?"

"We got." Toni smiled dryly. "There wasn't much else to do then. But I didn't believe she'd done it for a second. Neither had Gordon. Wade Lamont knew it. If we hadn't come along it would have been perfect. But we were the flaws. I wondered if he'd do anything about it. When Gordon Lazarus was killed today, I knew."

"Look," I said. "You say Wade was blackmailing Rickert. What for and why?"

"Because," she said, "Wade Lamont was desperately in love with Rickert's wife—Edith."

"A guy doesn't kill because he's in love. I never ran into love as a motive for murder in my life."

"That's like a man," Toni said. "I thought you were better than average but you're not. Love, my dear Candid Jones, is a wonderful thing—when *in* control. Out of control it can be as deadly as a cobra. Because love borders on hate often as not."

"I wouldn't know much about love," I said.

"Then I'm the key," she said. "Wade is crazy for Edith

Rickert. I know it. She's even told me. He's even proposed to her—proposed to a married woman! He told her to chuck Willie, that Willie was no good, didn't love her anymore. They had a terrible scene."

"Edith Rickert told you that?"

"Yes, and more. Now Wade Lamont was blackmailing Rickert not for money but by a threat of filthy publicity and scandal which would have wrecked not only Gladys' and Rickert's life, but also Edith's and maybe mine."

"Why you?"

"Rickert was backer of *Top Flight.*"

"Then he held Gladys' contracts."

"Yes." She smiled. "Why? Did you think I'd put a murder charge on her to get out of paying her a salary after the show flopped?"

"I'd considered it. Keep talking."

"WELL, LAMONT MADE Rickert keep his mouth shut, let him come and see Edith all he wanted to, let him make love to Edith, even tried to make him tell Edith to divorce him and marry Lamont. *That's* blackmail, my boy!"

"Finally," I said, finishing, "Rickert rebelled. Told Wade he was going to spill the whole dirty mess to Edith. Wade Lamont didn't want that because Edith Rickert would never have stomached him then. So he killed Rickert, dumped the rap on Gladys—and at the same time did what he'd wanted to do, cast a rotten stigma on Willie Rickert, so that Edith would loathe him, dead or alive, and would go to Lamont to be comforted and cheered."

"Candid," Toni said, "You are not bad at all. There is your case. What are you going to do about it?"

"Nothing," a new ominous voice broke in. "Not a thing, if you get what I mean."

My back was toward the door. I saw Toni Schulberg's eyes find the source of the voice and go pop-eyed in dismay and fear. I glanced at my watch. It read: 7:25 P.M. Then I slowly turned and as I did so, I eased the Lüger out of its holster and into my left hand so that by the time I had turned around fully, it was tight against my side, just above my waist and aimed on a straight line ahead of me.

"I get what you mean, boys," I said coldly, "but it's checkmate. Who starts the shooting?"

Something hard stabbed me in the small of the back on my left side, the muzzle of a gun, boring in. "Who starts the shooting?" Toni Schulberg asked in a voice that dripped icicles. "Maybe I'll start it, my dear Candid. Stand still."

I smiled. Over my shoulder, I said: "Toni, old thing, I wondered when you'd finally break down and pull that popgun on me. It's been making an awful bulge in your handbag for the last ten minutes."

Her voice didn't sound pretty anymore. "Don't give me that, sucker. You've been taken right and you know it."

"I haven't been taken," I said. "Not since I came home. Maybe before that I was on the fence because Wade Lamont *wasn't* a southpaw and I had to find one. I found one when I found you—even if we did convict Lamont rather nicely."

"You die hard," she said. "Drop the Lüger into the chair."

9

NEAT BUT NOT GAUDY

THE DOOR OF the studio was closed. Shep Coxe, covered with soup stains and looking sore as well, still covered me with his revolver—the same one he had shot Lazarus with. I saw it was a Smith & Wesson. It still had a silencer over the barrel. Phony Shapiro, looking bigger and fatter, had his pistol on my midriff. Only he didn't have his silencer in stock anymore. The jammed gun at the Warwick had cured him apparently. My watch said 7:28. There wasn't anything to do but stall. I dropped my Lüger into the chair.

"Against the wall with your hands up," Toni Schulberg said quietly.

I walked over to the wall opposite Coxe and Shapiro and put up my hands, facing them.

Toni picked up my Lüger and snapped off the safety and then she put her own gun, a little pearl-handled job, about .25 calibre, back into her bag, and she held my own rod on me—in her left hand, of course.

"Anything you want to say?" she asked, watching me sharply.

"Listen," Shep Coxe said, straightening his glasses, "let's skip the palaver and get this job over with. I never did like last words with a guy I was going to kill."

"You're not going to kill this one," Toni said. "I'm handling this one myself."

"With *that* cannon?" Shapiro exclaimed. "Listen, Toni, let Shep do it. That Lüger will sound like a construction company blasting. Shep's got the silencer. It works fair, even on a revolver. It stops some of the sound."

Toni's eyes half-closed. "All right," she said. "Hand me the gun, Shep."

Shep Coxe, grinning at not having to do the job himself, handed his gun to her. Phony Shapiro slipped his pistol into his pocket.

"He's got another gun on him," she said then. "Get it, boys."

Right then, I got the setup. I said sharply: "Wait a second—I haven't any gun—"

But that didn't stop them. Coxe and Shapiro walked over to me and started to frisk me when Toni Schulberg snapped: "All three of you—hands up!"

Coxe and Shapiro turned and stared at her. "For cat's sake, Toni—" Coxe started to say.

"Don't you get it, you dumb ginzos?" I said evenly. "We three are the only guys who know that she killed Willie Rickert. She'll plug you with my rod. And she'll plug me with Shep's rod. And it'll tell a swell story: SLEUTH SLAYS HOODS BUT DIES IN FIGHT HIMSELF!"

Coxe set his teeth. Shapiro grew very pale and under his swarthy skin, he looked green. "Toni—"

"That's the play, boys," Toni Schulberg said. "Anything else?"

"There are a few things on my mind," I said.

"No stalling," Toni said.

"No stalling," I said. "I've played ball. I want it cleared up before the payoff."

"You tell me, my dear Candid." She smiled thinly and waved the guns at me.

"All right," I said watching her trigger finger on the revolver which was meant for me. "You were the one who was blackmailing Rickert. You were threatening him with the juiciest scandal that ever rocked this man's town. When he said he was through and was going to expose you, you killed him. Your hate for Gladys Merwin made you throw the charge in her lap."

"You're very smart, my dear Candid. And why did I do all this?"

"There's only one answer," I said. "Not money. Not fear. Not passion. No—only one answer."

"Go ahead."

"LOVE," I SAID. "What you said about love being deadly as a cobra hit close to home. You killed Rickert and you framed Gladys because he was in love with her—*and she had taken him away from you!* Some guy once said that hell had no fury like a woman scorned. You tried to blackmail Rickert into coming back to you. He scorned you, I figure."

"Keep talking, smart guy."

"Lazarus went to the hotel with you. You must've told him what had happened—told him Gladys had killed Rickert. Whereas you shot Rickert from the door wearing evening gloves, no doubt, to kill prints on the pistol. And then you tossed the gun into the room and scrammed. Lazarus suspected you were lying. Maybe he tried to squeeze you. He wasn't safe. So you hired these two dopes to kill Lazarus for you. And they did."

"Keep talking," she said.

"Why, you even fooled a square guy like Clyde Simmons," I said. "You had him put me on the spot. You told him you were in danger, told him to send me home here where you were to get your story. And your story was only to be a bullet. What do you think, Toni? I'm pretty smart, eh?"

"So smart," she said between set teeth, "that you wind up dead."

"That's why Lazarus changed his story for Wade Lamont—told Wade that he was suing his wife for infidelity. Because Lazarus was playing ball with you and he expected to bleed you for plenty. You were the one who lifted the pistol from the property table backstage last night."

"Okay," Toni said, setting herself. "You've cleared up a few things and that's that. And now the joke's on you." She raised her guns steadily.

I laughed. "I've got a little joke too, my dear Toni," I said, mimicking her tone of voice. "And this little joke happens to be on you. I've recorded your little act. There is a 16mm motion picture camera in that corner to your left. It's wired for sound. The mike is in the photoflood reflector on your right. And this pretty scene has been put on gelatin since these two monkeys interrupted our tête-à-tête."

Toni gasped and she jerked her head around to look at the camera. It was four long strides to her. I took them fast. I didn't try for her guns. No chance. She heard me and she fired my Lüger before she even turned back to see me. But the bullet went wide.

I reached her with a sweeping right. I never hit anyone

so hard in my life. I caught her high, on the temple beside her left eye. I hurt my hand. There was a nasty crack and she went down harder than if a .45 had hit her.

I could tell that Coxe and Shapiro were in motion behind me. I dove for the Lüger and got it and I wheeled on my knees as Shapiro fired twice at me with his Colt pistol.

He missed me.

I shot once at him and I thought I got him but he rolled on the floor away and then to his feet.

Before I could get another try at him, Coxe hit me in a tackle and we both hit the floor all wrapped up in each other. I lost my gun.

Simultaneously the studio door flew open. I saw Rentano and Soho McLean coming in. They had their Police Positives out but they didn't shoot. I saw Soho McLean jump Phony Shapiro's pistol. It was as courageous an act as a guy ever pulled. It wasn't done fast. McLean just sort of trotted up to Shapiro and he did it so neatly, Shapiro was too stunned to even fire. And the next thing, he took McLean's barrel across the head and collapsed.

Rentano was trying to get a bead on Shep Coxe. But there was none of that. I had my own troubles. Coxe was hitting me low and there wasn't much I could do about it. We both struggled for the other rod—the revolver with the silencer which Toni Schulberg dropped when I hit her. Coxe got it.

He was a tall guy, Coxe was. A head over me. When he got that gun, he jerked me to my feet, facing him, and he stuck that gun past me at Rentano and snarled: "Away from the door you! No copper's taking me! Get away from that door and drop your heaters or I'll plug this lily where he stands!"

THERE WAS A split-second silence. I couldn't see, but I could feel that Rentano was dumfounded; he didn't know what to do. The same with McLean. If they tried for Shep Coxe, they thought it'd be curtains for Candid Jones.

I didn't like the idea but it was the only thing to do. With my right hand, I reached up into my sleeve and pulled down the plunger there, and then I pressed the plunger in with my thumb.

The report wasn't very loud. My clothes muffled it. Shep Coxe dropped his gun. He put his hand to his chest and opened his mouth to say something. But he didn't say anything. He dropped to the floor and laid very still, his eyes still open and his mouth still fixed to speak.

"O.K., boys," I said to Rentano and McLean.

I bent down and had a look. Coxe was dead. It was tough luck in a way. I hadn't wanted to kill him. But you see, he was a tall guy. And it so happened that his heart was on a direct line with the Simplex Pockette camera-gun which was strapped under my right armpit.

That's what happened.

"How much did you hear?" I asked Rentano.

"I heard plenty!" he cried.

"She," Soho McLean snorted, "was a lulu if I've ever seen one." He glared at Toni Schulberg on the floor.

"You heard it all," I said. "You've got to be sure of that."

"Listen," said Rentano, "Gladys'll be out of the can before tonight or else. When the D.A. sinks his teeth in this bunch of words—besides you've got the camera and the sound pictures. We heard you."

I sighed. "Hell, no. That was just a bluff to take down her guard."

"Doesn't matter," Rentano said. "She'll be out tonight. And a hell of a fine job, Candid. Let's get these two live ones down to h.q., Soho. And call the wagon for the other stiff… How'd you lamp her motive, Candid?"

"I guessed it," I said. I felt pretty tired. "You heard the rest. There's not much evidence."

"Hell with evidence," said Soho McLean. "That's just a fallacy anyhow. I've been a cop for thirty years. It's always been my theory. Find the guy who did it. Slap him in the jug. Spread his pictures around, make people think he's guilty. Let the D.A. worry about the details. And ten to one your killer fries in the chair. But she won't be much trouble. She'll talk her head off when she comes around. That's the trouble with women—always ready to talk."

I looked up at him and I grinned. "That reminds me of something," I said. "I believe I promised you a wallop."

"The day she got out," Soho McLean said. "I guess this is the day all right."

"How'd he happen to come along?" I asked Rentano.

Rentano replied: "I called him after you telephoned. He wanted to come along."

Soho McLean sighed. "I've been wrong before, son. I admit I was wrong this morning. I've got it coming to me for what I said. So take your sock."

I grinned at him and shook my head. "Not me. I wouldn't hit a guy who jumps a gun like that. Suppose we shake instead."

"Now that's what I been wanting to hear," Soho McLean said, a slow, glinty smile spreading over his grizzled cheeks.

"As a matter of fact, I kind o' like your style, Candid. It's—well—it's like a newspaper bulletin. Clipped. You know. Neat but not—uh—"

"Gaudy?" Rentano said.

"That's it," Soho McLean said, misunderstanding Rentano, and glancing at Toni Schulberg on the floor, and Shep Coxe and Phony Shapiro on the floor. "That's it exactly. Neat but not gory."

Inspector Rentano looked at me, his eyes twinkling at McLean's mistake, but he didn't say anything.

MURDER ON THE FILM

Candid Jones, Camera-Toting Ex-Dick, Places His Shots With a Lüger and Leica Where They Do the Most Good

1

MURDER—WITH PICTURES

I WAS COMING out of the stage door of the Merivale Theater on West 47th Street when I saw a small dumpy man turn into the stage door alley. I was carrying my Leica Model G under my top coat against the right side of my chest and there was a brand new cartridge-roll of supersensitive film in it—enough, for thirty-six exposures.

The little fat man saw me. He saw me, but he didn't pay any attention to me. He came into the alley fast, in a skipping sort of step, like a tipsy ballet dancer, but he hadn't gone more than ten feet before I heard the two shots.

For a moment, he froze there, utterly lifeless, as though his whole body had been dipped into frigid liquid air.

Then his eyes opened very wide, as though they were seeing something very horrible, and he threw up his hands over his head and finally, he spun around twice, with infinite slowness and care. Then he toppled over. I thought he'd never hit the pavement. He seemed to float through the air with the greatest of ease, as though he were actually controlling the speed of his fall all by himself.

I didn't even think about doing it; the whole thing came automatically. But before that guy hit the ground, I had two

"Slack that finger,
Durken!" said Candid

pictures of him at 1/500th of a second and I knew when I
shot them he was dead.

Jake Brand, who was producing *Heads Up*, the musical
which was due to open that same night at the Merivale, had
given me a call earlier that morning, a Wednesday, to run
down and take some publicity shots of his dress rehearsal.
I'd arrived at two-fifteen and I'd taken around a hundred
photos or so of the cast and principals in action. Mostly,
I'd put Jane Rickert's face on negatives. Jane Rickert was
the star of *Heads Up*—a sweet, unspoiled kid who could
dance like Marilyn Miller had, could sing like "Moon-
Glow" Langford. I mean she was all right.

When I'd finished the shooting at the Merivale, I'd
loaded the Leica again, just in case, and I'd set it at its
hyper-focal distance stop with the lens at f/8—and I was
heading for my studio uptown when I ran into the little
fat man.

It was just lucky, my grabbing those two shots, because
f/8 was a perfect lens opening in that alley's light.

When the fat man hit the ground, I dropped the Leica
and it swung back under my coat, suspended on its strap

Rentano turned the tables

around my neck. And then I started running toward the guy.

I didn't reach him first. The man who'd killed him did. He got there so unexpectedly, he stopped me dead in my tracks. He ducked into the alley and knelt down over the fat man's corpse. If it hadn't been for the Smith and Wesson .38 revolver in his left hand, I'd have thought he was an interested passerby.

Not that boy. He reached into a pocket—a special pocket which indicated he knew what he was doing—and when his hand came out, he had an envelope.

He stuffed it in his coat as he got to his feet. That's when I got him with the Leica. And I got him right. He wasn't more than twenty feet away.

HE DIDN'T HEAR any camera click, but he saw me move and as he turned to glance at me, he realized I had a camera. He was a man of decision. He didn't beat about the bush. He let go three bullets at me like the snap of a finger and the crack of the gun made a hell of a racket in that alley.

None of the slugs nicked me, but that didn't make any

difference. The fourth one might have, so I did a nose-dive for his benefit and stiffened when I hit the ground, wondering if he'd make another try.

He didn't.

Before I could even turn my head, a car roared up to the curb, a voice as deep as a bullfrog said calmly: "Hug the crate, Frenchy, we're leaving here. The flatfoot's on his way down the block."

"I got it," Frenchy said. "Step on it." Another roar and the car was gone, and the killer with the Smith and Wesson was gone too, leaving the fat man lying there dead, and me lying there flat on my back.

I was on my knees, trying to catch my breath after the way things happened, when the flatfoot arrived. He didn't pay any attention to either me or the body, but he stood framed outside the alley and he poured out every bullet his Police Positive had in its chambers.

When it clicked emptily, he made a terrible face and I knew he had missed. Then he put his gun away and ran into the alley. He saw me leaning against the wall and he cried: "Have they nicked ye, lad?"

I said: "No, I'm all right. Better look the fat boy over."

"Aye," the cop said. "But it's little use to be doin' that for he's never to be deader."

We moved over to the fat man and turned him over, for he'd fallen on his face. There was a bad bruise on his cheek where he'd hit, but otherwise his skin was that pale waxy saffron color. It's unique because it paints death. You can't mistake it.

The corpse's neck was flecked with blood where a slug had torn through. But that wasn't the shot which had killed him. The two droopy lines of blood which hung from the corners of the pallid lips indicated a stomach wound. There was no finding the hole under a suit and an overcoat—not in that alley.

In the street, a crowd was beginning to gather. I figured the flatfoot was going to have his troubles pushing off the morbid idlers and trying to guard his corpse at the same time. Also I figured I didn't want to stand around there just then and answer questions.

"Look, officer," I said. "You wait here with this stiff and I'll call Rentano at h.q. and give him the bad news."

"I WAS EXPECTIN' a brother policeman," said the cop, looking harassed, "but ye can never find a cop when you need one." He said it unconsciously, not realizing the humor of it. Then he jerked his head around and stared hard at me. "Ye sound familiar with Inspector Rentano," he added, scowling. "Would ye be knowin' him, lad?"

"Faith, yes!" I said, imitating his thick brogue and grinning at him. "I was pulling Harry Rentano's leg when he was still a sergeant up in Highbridge."

He still staged at me. "Red hair, freckles…" he muttered. "And that long nose—ye have a familiar air, lad. I seem to remember—"

I said: "They use to call me Candid Jones when I was gumshoe for the Apex Insurance Company."

"By the saints!" he exploded. "Candid Jones. The hard-boiled shamus—ye look so young, lad!"

"I'll telephone Rentano," I said.

"By all means," said the cop. "And tell him to send Black Maria. This gentleman will be takin' his next to last ride when he heads for the morgue."

I went back into the Merivale Theater and I found the phone booth by the stage door and stepped into it. The girls of the chorus were still on the stage ironing out a routine and apparently nobody there knew anything had gone wrong. I dropped a nickel in the slot and called Centre Street and when they answered, I asked for Inspector Harry Rentano.

I'd known Rentano pretty well in the days before I quit sleuthing for the Apex Company in 1932. I had had to stick my nose into plenty of police business because Apex insured anything that was worth money and crooks didn't hijack small change. It was grand larceny most of the time; two guys you could always expect on the scene were Rentano and Candid Jones. That was before he was shifted to the homicide squad.

Rentano was a white man all the way. As a cop, he was smart, tactful, and courageous. Sometimes a little too damn fearless. I often figured that when he broke up the Mafia single-handed, he'd had a lot of luck to come out of the mêlée alive; because a lone hand on that kind of job was asking for a bump-off. But he did it. And his work on the Bomb Squad had made that detail famous, especially during the hectic week when some lunatic mailed a lot of time bombs to important boys in Wall Street. That was a week that almost matched the famous Wall Street bombing.

But outside of being the best detective on the force, Rentano was a swell guy—as a human being, I meant. He had a great wife, Katie Rentano, who was not a bit hard to look at; and he had four kids, two boys and two girls.

I figured that when I quit the shamus racket to go into

commercial photography, I'd drop out of touch with Rentano and all the other guys I'd known. As a matter of fact,
most of the yeggs were just as glad I left the racket. I'd had
a rep in those days for speaking frankly and acting frankly.
That's where I picked up the moniker "Candid."

But Rentano kept track of me. He used to visit me at the
studio on Fifth Avenue, and once he brought the beauteous
Kate along for me to make a portrait.

"Hello?" He said suddenly, then, "who is it?" His voice
was clear and low and it had volume that could be heard
out on the stage of the theater.

"Hello, Harry," I said quietly. "This is Candid."

"Who?"

"Candid Jones," I said. "I'm calling from the Merivale
on West 47th Street."

"Well, for God's sake," Rentano said, sounding as though
his face were set in a smirk; "I thought you'd taken it on the
lam for Tahiti or something. I haven't seen you since we got
your ex-wife out of that very pretty jam—"

I said: "Look, Harry. I was lying low. I didn't like the way
the tabs were pulling me back into the detective racket. I
told you once I'd quit for good. I meant that—"

"Candid, my lad," Rentano replied with sarcasm, "you
are speaking the juice of a prune. In other words, you're a
sap. Why, being a hard-knuckled dick comes easy to you.
It's your life's work and you can't get away from it by will-
power. I'm not saying you aren't a good camera man. But
you just can't stomach crime, kiddo. It's in your blood. And
if you were smart, you'd—"

I heave a long sigh for him and I said: "If you'll stop
kibitzing long enough to let me sling a word in here, I'll tell

you why I called. A guy was just bumped off in the stage door alley of the Merivale. I saw it. I saw the guy who did it and I took some pictures. I don't want to get mixed up with a lot of questions and answers out front, so I'm calling you and tipping you off. After you look the scene over here, run uptown to the studio and I'll have the pictures ready for you. Got that?"

"Kiddo," Rentano breathed, "you're miraculous. I'll see you in half an hour."

I hung up, left the Merivale by the front door, and rode a hack east toward Fifth. Nobody, including the perspiring cop, saw me go.

2

COP IN YOUR BLOOD

CAMERA IS A funny thing. You sight it and you take a picture and you've made a record of a phase of life—or maybe death. You can make evidence with it by grabbing the right shot. You can squat a guy in the electric chair with a slice of negative properly exposed. You can even fake a composite picture and scare a smart boy into spilling the beans, like I did with Alex Wolfe when he was up to his neck in the Bojangles horse-race affair.

Yeah, a camera is a great thing when it takes the right kind of pictures. And the way they make the minicams today—the Leica, the Contax, the Wirgen—you can just about take a picture of a coal chunk against a sepia background at midnight.

But there's one thing you can't do with a camera, no matter how good the thing is or how much it cost.

You can't take a picture when the lens is covered.

That's what I'd done. Me making the amateur's prime mistake. It was a laugh. It was the saddest kind of laugh a man can make. But it was a fact.

Everything had happened so quickly in that alley, I'd snapped my shutter without realizing that I'd put my lens cap over the Summar lens. A lens cap is a circular leather piece which covers the glass entirely, keeping out the dust and preventing the lens from being scratched carelessly.

I only found it out after I'd put the film in the developer. It came out denser than a moron. I took a look at the camera. There was the lens cap.

Inspector Harry Rentano arrived at the studio a few minutes later. I was pacing around when he opened the door. I felt like a fool and I was wondering what I was going to tell him....

"Hello, kiddo," he said, coming in and closing the door with a slam. He stood there a second and smiled at me. He looked the same. He was smoking a miniature cigar and he looked short and broad, and you could see that he still had the muscle, even if he'd put on weight below his chest. He wore a blue overcoat and a black derby and the semi-circular white scar above his right eye where he'd once been knifed, was plainly visible.

"Hello, Harry," I said. "Grab a chair."

"Sure," he said, sitting down over by the studio camera, pushing a photo-flood reflector aside so that he could stretch out his legs. "You're looking the same. Only I will say you're homelier if anything."

I smiled weakly.

"You've got more freckles," he said. "How in hell do you pick 'em up anyhow? You probably haven't seen the sun in months. And that schnozzola—ye gods—"

"Lay off," I said.

Rentano smiled slyly. "Still get sore when the nose is kidded, heh?"

I didn't answer him on that. "You don't look worried," I

said. "Or isn't this your particular case. I suppose you've given it to Bill Hanley."

"Uh-uh," said Rentano. "As a matter of fact, Poppa Hanley has a homicide of his own that's giving him a headache. But why should I be worried?"

I said: "You mean you know who bumped—"

"Me? No. But you do. You said you got a picture of the punk who did it."

I LIGHTED A cigarette and I sat down beside him. "It'll probably be a blow to you," I said. "There are no pictures." And I told him in detail what had happened.

His face changed. It began to droop. He said: "That's kind of a blow, Candid. I'd counted on those snaps."

"No use crying over spilt milk."

"It's not a matter of spilt milk," Rentano muttered, chewing more savagely on his cigar now. "The thing is this: Callahan—the cop you met back at the Merivale— he didn't see a damn thing. How could he? He was down the block when he heard the shots and he came running, that's all. I figured—"

"I didn't see much myself," I said. "The guy who shot the fat man was nicknamed Frenchy. I heard that much. But even if Frenchy let a couple of slugs out in the open after me, I didn't see much of his face. I was busy ducking."

"You don't know what he looked like, Candid?"

"No," I said. "He wore a brown plaid cap which fell off and he had on a gray top-coat. But I didn't see his face. I tell you, they called him Frenchy. Doesn't that help you out?"

Rentano looked hurt. "Oh, tremendously," he said. "A big help. There's only one Frenchy in town I know. I can put my finger right on him. His moniker's Frenchy LaSeur. He's a killer. He works for Phil Durken's crowd."

I shrugged. "There you are."

"There *you* are," Rentano sighed. "He'll have an airtight alibi or else he'll have died an hour before the thing came off. Phil Durken doesn't fool around, Candid. He covers his men."

"I don't seem to remember a Phil Durken."

"He's come up since you quit the racket. He covers the field. Blackmail, whitemail, confidence stuff. The works. He's organized. Trying to convict one of his men is like looking for a needle in a haystack."

"Well, how do you like that?" I said with sarcasm. "You just about know that Frenchy LaSeur bumped off the guy, and you look worried. I know one way of getting that guy to talk. And it isn't with a powder puff either. Are you going soft, Harry?"

Rentano shook his head thoughtfully and didn't answer me. He spoke at random. "No use. Just beat him up. Get a confession. And what? Alibi would kick the confession outa court. You know who the guy was who died? The little fat man?"

I shook my head.

"Pat McCoy," said Rentano.

I looked shocked. I lighted a cigarette to cover up my face and I walked to the window and looked out and down into the traffic... "I didn't recognize him," I said. "He'd gotten much fatter. But I hadn't seen him in four years. It's tough."

It was more than tough but I didn't feel like talking about it. I was getting a little hot under the collar and I knew that if I opened up, Rentano would provoke me into saying something foolish—like helping him on the case.

I didn't want that. I wanted to steer clear of the gumshoe racket. I'd had enough of that when I knocked off in 1932. But when I was mad, it was hard to stay away. And I was mad just then.

"Pat McCoy," Rentano grated. "An ex-cop. You know what that means?"

I nodded. It meant that the police department would rip things wide open until they laid it on the right guy.

"You can't kill a cop," I said quietly, "and get away with it in this burg."

Rentano sighed. "Used to be that way. Times seem to have changed. The way those shysters wangle the Law nowadays—"

"Getting late," I said, avoiding the topic and staring out the window.

"Look, Candid—"

"No, Harry. Skip it. I'm through. I'm not coming back. If I came back once more, I'd come back to stay."

"SURE! YOU DAMNED fool! You'll stay. You *should* stay. You've got cop in your blood. You were born that way. And you'll never get it out of you. Pat McCoy was retired when he reached his pension age. But would he quit? Hell, no. He was a cop, too. And he stayed. You know what he did? He opened up a one-man private detective agency. And what's more he was making a go of it. He was working on a case for a client when he got bumped off. You like that?"

"I'm sorry those pictures didn't come out," I said coldly. "Now lay off. You're pushing me, Harry. You're pushing me all over the place. I don't like it. Now cut it out and let's stay friends."

Rentano threw up his hands and came over and hit me on the back. "Forget it, kiddo. I don't mean to lay it on so hard. But it breaks my heart to see a guy like you taking pictures for a living. Candid Jones—the only shamus who ever made Al Capone tip his hat. Oh well…" He went through the door and his voice floated back over his shoulder. "I'll give you a ring if anything turns up."

"Remember me to Katie," I called. And the door closed.

3

THERE WAS A CROOKED MAN—

I HAD MADE a date with Jane Rickert of *Heads Up* to take her to the White Slipper Club for dining and dancing. As a matter of fact, I hadn't really made it. She made it. I liked her all right, more than I should have, maybe, and when I'd been at the Merivale, I'd suggested that we get together sometime, and she'd said: "Fine. Tonight's the night, Candid. I'm not doing a thing."

And that's how it had happened.

It meant top hat—white tie—tails. I hadn't been into my monkey suit in so long, I almost didn't know how to put the thing on. And all the time, I thought of Pat McCoy. When I put my studs in my shirt, when I put on the strap-around vest, I couldn't get Pat McCoy out of my mind. Nor could I forget Harry Rentano's words: *"You've got cop in your blood."*

Rentano was right, of course, even if I didn't want to admit it. I was boiling, deep down inside myself, and for two pins I'd have gone out after Frenchy LaSeur and if I hadn't been able to pin the thing on him legally, I'd have shot it out with him.

You see, the whole thing hinged on Pat McCoy. Ordinarily, you'd say it was all part of the game. A plain and simple murder and a killer to be caught. But with Pat

McCoy, dumpy, short and fat, it was different. Forty years a cop. From patrolman to lieutenant. A jovial little man with white hair and blue Irish eyes.

The kids of the Tenth Precinct had known Pat McCoy. For when the Yuletide season rolled around and there were kids and kids whose family didn't have a red cent to buy them a doll or a train, it was the cops of the force who chipped in and paid for the toys. And it was smiling Pat McCoy who played Santa Claus. They used to deck him out in the familiar red suit with the white fur and he'd distribute the presents to all the youngsters. Play Santa Claus?

No. Pat McCoy didn't have to play the part. He *was* Santa Claus. He not only looked like that venerable old gent—glistening red cheeks, laughing eyes, white hair— but many was the time he'd split his own pay envelope with a family who needed the money as badly as he himself no doubt did.

And I stood there, staring at myself in the mirror while I dressed and I thought: "Look at you. Hard-boiled Jones. Candid Jones of the Lüger and the brass knuckles. You've got a tear in your eye when you think of that Irish Santa Claus mick. You feel so badly about it your throat's all swollen with a lump like an egg. Soft, that's it. The guy without sentiment going soft."

But I knew I couldn't go on that way. I couldn't go back to crime again. There was nothing I'd rather have done than gone after Pat McCoy's killer. But if I went back once more, it would be to stay. I knew I'd be gone after that. I'd be a dick again.

"Nope. No more of that," I said to myself. "That's all washed up. *Fini.*"

The voice of Rentano reminded me: You've got cop in your blood.

"Nix," I said aloud to myself. "No more of that stuff." And I put on my glistening top hat, got my gloves and stick and left the studio. Jane Rickert lived over on Central Park West. I whistled a cruising hack over to the curb, got in, and gave the driver Jane's address.

But as it turned out, I didn't get to take Jane Rickert anywhere, and this is what happened.

She lived at a beautiful apartment house, Jane did. Just below 81st Street. The long green canopy with its indirect lighting had the name of the place on the wavy fringes: Hawthorne Arms. I paid off the driver when I got there and I got out with the corsage I'd picked up at a florist's on the way and I took the elevator up to the eighth floor.

When I got out two men were leaving her apartment. The maid, a perky-little Irisher who tried to put on a French accent, was at the door with them. She was plainly disturbed, since she said adamantly and with a touch of both French and Irish brogue: "Please *messieurs,* you will kindly leave, *n'est-ce pas?* Or, faith, I'll lay a brickbat across yer skulls!"

The men laughed harshly and raucously, one punching the other in the ribs with an elbow in a gesture of amusement. Then the maid slammed the door and that was that. **THE ELEVATOR HAD** gone down by then. The two men still stood at the door. I went up to it, past them, and I reached out my hand to ring the doorbell. Instantly, it was snatched away by one of the two guys, and the guy who'd done the snatching laughed out loud.

I turned slowly and took a short-long look at both of them. The big one had a crooked face. One side of it was straight. The other side absolutely lopsided. The nose went crooked in the center of its bridge. His mouth went crooked on the left side. He had a small red scar under his right cheek-bone which made his cheek there go down crookedly toward the lobe of his left ear.

His hair was quite gray where it showed under his black fedora, and his grin disclosed a set of teeth that shined with a dull yellow glow in the light of the foyer there. His ears hung down very low, the lobes not far above his neck. And he had big black pores around his nose and chin.

"Well!" he said, his voice a familiar frog-bass which I'd heard before. "Well—all dressed up and no place to go, eh, Dude? Ain't you ashamed runnin' around like this—like a big sissy?" And he roared, laughing.

"I've got places to go," I said, watching his eyes. "Take your hand off my arm."

The second man was extremely thin and I recognized him simultaneously, although the full dress outfit didn't let him place me for several seconds. Red-eyed, long and haggard face, it was Willy-Nilly Baker, a small-time hood I'd once nabbed when he tried to break a jewelry store on 14th Street—insured by Apex—back in 1926. I'd seen him a lot after he got out of stir again. He looked the same.

"Did you hear the Dude?" the crooked man laughed boisterously as he held his grip on my arm. "He wants me to let him go."

Willy-Nilly Baker, hardly glancing at me, laughed shortly and nodded toward the elevator. "Let's blow, Phil."

"Sure, sure," the crooked man said slowly. He watched me very carefully and he raised his free hand with a forefinger extended, as though he were about to reprove a small boy. "Now, now, Dude. You listen to teacher. You ain't got places to go tonight. Not with Miss Rickert. She ain't feelin' so good right now and she wants to be alone."

"Take your hand off my arm," I said evenly.

He tightened his grip and yanked me close to him, his eyes blazing. "Mustn't use that tone o' voice to Popper or he's liable to spank," he snapped. "Take it on the lam, Dude. I'm sick o' seein' you. And don't be back—"

"You asked for it," I said.

I drove my free left into his stomach, short and hard with my full weight behind it. The crooked man had a bit of a paunch there and it was very soft. I felt my fist go all the way in until it must have scraped his spine.

He let out a woof, went double, let go my arm, and sat down very neatly on the floor.

WILLY-NILLY BAKER LOOKED stunned. His hand went up to a shoulder holster and stopped there. Then the crooked man recovered his breath enough to paw for a .45 pistol which he got out. I saw the safety was on and the crooked man was unnerved enough not to be able to locate it with his thumb.

I cracked the back of his wrist with my stick and picked up the gun when it dropped. Then while he struggled toward his feet, I hit him again. Behind the ear. He sat down again, then laid down, out cold.

I wheeled on Willy-Nilly Baker with the crooked man's

pistol—it was a Colt—all ready to go. But Willy-Nilly was just staring and his mouth hung agape and his eyes were frightened.

"Hello, Willy-Nilly." I said.

His mouth moved; no sound came out at all, except the sticky cluck of his tongue against the saliva in his cheek.

"Are you drawing on me?" I asked.

"Gawd!" he whistled then. "Not me, not me—" He caught his breath in a noisy inhalation. "Ain't you—you're not—?"

I said quietly: "Red hair, Willy-Nilly. And freckles. And the nose you never could afford to make a crack about."

"*Candid Jones!*" And unconsciously he tipped his hat.

I asked him who his friend was, the crooked man on the floor who was breathing hard, utterly inert, a red spot under his ear.

"Phil—Phil Durken," Willy-Nilly said, faltering.

As if in response to his name, the man on the floor stirred, rubbing the spot where I'd clipped him. Presently, he sat up.

I said: "Where does he hang out?"

Willy-Nilly said: "The—you mean—yeah, he lives at the Colonial on Broadway."

"He would." I said. "And I figure I can find a punk named Frenchy LaSeur there too?"

"You might," said Willy-Nilly.

"Help me up," Durkin growled suddenly, struggling to his feet. "I'm goin' to kill that creampuff if it's the last thing—"

"Shut your trap," said Willy-Nilly Baker. "Don't tackle with this bird. He's a walking arsenal and you'll come out feet first. He's got rods all over him and they go off at funny times and from funny places. He's poison, Phil—listen to me and don't go off on an ear—"

"I don't care who he is!"

I smiled at Durkin coldly and I handed him back his Colt pistol. He snatched it out of my hand and the damned fool actually tried to kill me there in the foyer. He triggered the gun and after the first empty click, he stopped, looking asinine and he gasped: "You lifted the clip."

"I lifted the clip," I said. "I'm not giving away my life, Durkin. I'm not quite the Santa Claus Pat McCoy used to be."

"Who are you anyhow?" Durkin asked icily, the gun still in his hand.

"Candid Jones," I said, "I'm the guy Frenchy LaSeur shot down and killed when he got Pat McCoy this afternoon. I'm the guy who took the pictures of Frenchy killing McCoy. I'm the guy who took the pictures of Durkin in the car that picked up Frenchy LaSeur. In other words—I'm the guy—and not dead by a damned sight. Durken! And the pictures, my friend, were lovely. You will see them in all good time."

"I NEVER HEARD of you," Durkin said. But his face was pale from what he'd heard. "And I don't know nothin' about Pat McCoy and you never took no pictures or anything. But I'll tell you this, wise guy. The next time I see you I'll have slugs in this rod. And I'll kill you on sight."

"Sure," I said slowly, "unless I kill you first. Take your friend home, Willy-Nilly, and tell him the facts of life. And any time he wants to play cops and robbers, let me know. I'm right in the phone book, and the Lüger is well-oiled."

Durken turned around, a queer new look on his face that I couldn't fathom. Willy-Nilly Baker turned too, but he said: "Take it easy, Candid. Now take it easy." And he tipped his hat. Then they both stepped into the elevator when it came up, and they were gone.

I took a deep breath and had to laugh in relief. Baker's crack about my being a walking arsenal was really funny. Outside of the clip of bullets I'd taken from Phil Durken's gun—a clip without a weapon to use them in—I was as naked of artillery as a new-born baby.

I felt pretty good that I'd got out of the business alive.

You can bluff so far with a rat, then you have to use the dukes or fade. Bluff is great stuff and so is a front. I was proud of that hard-boiled front. It goes a long way. But comes the day when a rat will scare into panic, and then the front is only seen in its real light—an illusion. Then you put up your dukes and wade. And if the duke's don't work—bullets have to do the job.

I've got to admit I never had any scruples about killing a man. Inspector Harry Rentano once told me I was cold-blooded about it. But I'm not. I don't like to kill; it's not a lust or obsession. I don't like it any more than the average man. But when it's my life against a rat's. I like to play safe. I don't feel any regret. I don't feel squeamish when I kill a guy who's going to try and kill me sooner or later. It seems the cleanest way in the end. So many of the punks can beat the law. They can't beat a slug.

I rang the bell to Jane Rickert's apartment and I waited a long time before Mary, the maid ("Marie" in her French moods), opened up. Her nose was as sharp as a razor and she looked up at me over the end of it with fire in her eyes and she spat: "What is it?"

"Miss Rickert was expecting me," I said.

"Oh," the maid said. "You're Mr. Jones."

"Terrence Jones," I said.

Instantly she softened. "You had the look of an Irishman. Come in, sir. Although I'm afraid Miss Rickert—she's not well—I'll tell her you're here."

I went in. Jane Rickert had a beautiful apartment. Her living room was in white. White leather, white fur, white bear rug. It was gorgeous. I'd never seen a layout like it anywhere. Everywhere you turned, a mirror hit you in the eye and you saw yourself. Just like an actress, I chuckled. I had a seat.

In a few seconds, she was out in the room with me.

I had the shock of my life when I saw her.

THE PALLOR OF death was on her cheeks. Her mouth, so red and desirable a few hours or so before, was lifeless, bloodless, touched with terror. The scourge seemed to have drained all beauty from her—a paradox if you could have seen her, for there wasn't a more beautiful girl in all show business. Her golden hair was as flat-hued as dull steel. No sparkle, no usual twinkle, her lovely eyes had pulled down gray shades over the rich depths of her irises.

"Jane," I said. "Come out of it."

"I'm—"

"What's the matter with you? You look terrible."

She smiled wanly, then burst into tears. I put my arm around her and put her in a chair but she wouldn't open up. She dried her eyes and looked worse. And I realized she was in negligee and had no intention of keeping the dancing date. Mary stood by with a bottle of smelling salts.

"Don't take on so, Miss Jane," Mary said. "It'll work out all right."

"What will work out?" I asked.

Jane raised her head. "I'm being beastly to you, Candid. I'm awfully sorry. I—I'm sure I can't make it with you this evening."

"Oh, to hell with that," I said. "I knew that when I saw you. That doesn't make any difference."

"That's good of you, Candid. Perhaps another time—I feel so wretched tonight—"

"Oh," I said. I watched her. "You don't feel well. That's all it is, eh?"

She nodded, biting her mouth hard.

I shrugged. "You're a bad liar. Suppose you give me the lowdown. Maybe I can help you out."

She sighed heavily. Mary moved toward me with my top hat but I waved her back and gave a look to show I meant it and she retreated. I pointed a forefinger at Jane Rickert. "How about it?"

"Candid, dear," she said quietly, "you're a nice young man whom I know very slightly, a chap who takes excellent pictures and has the gift of disarming frankness."

I smiled coldly. "But not big enough to handle your present dilemma, I take it?"

"I'm sorry," she said. "I didn't mean to be rude—"

"Then I'll be rude. I don't like the company you keep."

Her eyes went wide. "What are you talking about?"

"Phil Durken and Willy-Nilly Baker," I said. "A pair of rats. They had a man killed this afternoon—"

"Pat McCoy!" she breathed in horror.

I got up. I admit I was a little surprised. I'd been putting two and two together but I hadn't added up this. "You mean—you were the one—Pat McCoy was working on an assignment for you?"

She didn't answer. She didn't have to. Obviously he had been. Arriving there at the Merivale with that manila envelope. Being shot by LaSeur who took the envelope. Then Durkin and Baker visiting McCoy's client. It was a very pretty picture.

"YOU'RE BEING BLACKMAILED," I said, taking a shot in the dark, and when I heard her smothered gasp I knew it was a bull's-eye, and went on: "Durkin is blackmailing you. Somebody else was blackmailing you before that. You hired Pat McCoy to stop it. McCoy did. What was it in the envelope—letters?" She nodded dumbfounded. "Letters. McCoy got them back. But McCoy was shot and killed. And now Durken has the letters and he's squeezing you."

"I can't tell you anything—anything at all!" Jane Rickert cried. "They'll kill me if I do!"

"Please go—please—" she was breathing heavily. "You know too much, Candid. They'd kill me and you too if—how *could* you know?"

"I used to be a detective," I said dryly. "Correspondence school, you know. Diploma and all." I shrugged. "If you want to pay out, it's okay with me. I know the man who can help you out, though."

"Wh-who?"

"Inspector Rentano."

"A policeman? No! I—no publicity! I couldn't stand publicity! It could ruin the whole thing—"

"Sure," I said. "I understand. You wouldn't mind telling who the first one was—the first guy who was blackmailing you before Phil Durkin muscled in?"

"I can't. I can't say a word."

"I'll say this," I continued. "When Phil Durkin scares them, they seem to scare proper. This apartment faces the front doesn't it? It looks down on the Park?" And when she nodded, "Mind if I take a look from the bedroom? It's dark in there and I won't be seen."

We went in. I pulled back the curtains and peered down. I took a long look because I wanted to be certain. I couldn't see any tails down there. But that didn't mean a thing.

Oh, well, I figured, Brodie took a chance.

I picked up Jane Rickert's handset and I called h.q. and asked for the homicide bureau. The guy who answered sounded screwy. "Hi-ho," he said. "It's your nickel so start slinging English, my fran. Who died and why do you want Poppa Hanley?"

"It so happens," I replied, "that I don't want Poppa Hanley. Who is this anyhow?"

"The *Chronicle's* claim to fame," he replied. "Daffy Dill in the flesh. Yea verily."

"O.K., Dizzy," I said, "give me Inspector Rentano."

There were clicks. Daffy Dill faded. I could see why he was there. Rentano had said that Hanley was working on a homicide of his own. Naturally, Daffy Dill would have been with Hanley. Then a new voice broke in, and it was Harry Rentano.

"This is Candid, Harry."

"Hello, kiddo. I've got news for you."

"It'll keep," I said. "Meet me at my studio in twenty minutes or so, eh?"

"I'll be there ahead of you," he said and we both hung up.

4

THE GUMSHOE TRAIL—FOR KEEPS

CENTRAL PARK, ACROSS the way, was dark with the night when I reached the sidewalk in front of Jane Rickert's apartment house. The black stretch of it, studded with twinkling lights and sometimes flecked with the probing amber fingers of automobile headlights, was dipped in a faint mist which clung to the street lights like white fuzz.

I felt a trifle foolish in my evening clothes, foolish because I didn't have the girl to go with them.

The doorman moved toward me, smiling politely. "Taxi, sir?"

"Yeah," I said. "Taxi."

But before he'd had a chance to toot his little whistle for a cruising taxicab, the thing I'd been wary of happened. Two men moved out of the shadows to the right of the canopy with its Hawthorne Arms legend. Two men I'd never seen before in my life. I didn't know who they were but I knew what they wanted. They looked like the Siamese twins, both the same squat height, both wearing dark overcoats and dark snap-brims. But the similarity changed with their faces. For one had a placid moon-face, and the other a beetle-browed, ex-pug face.

Moon-face moved between me and the doorman with

a genial smile and he was careful to place himself so that the doorman could not see his face—nor the blue-steel Colt .32 which Pug-Face stuck into the muscles of my stomach. "Candid Jones!" Moon-Face cried as though pleasantly surprised. "This is a real treat. Haven't seen you in a dog's age!"

Pug-Face prodded me with the pistol and I played ball. "Why Mike," I said cheerfully. "You old rat." And I emphasized the "rat."

"You don't needa cab," Pug-Face growled, a poor actor at best. "We got the buggy right over here. We'll be glad to drop you anywheres you say, Candid."

"That'll be fine, won't it, Candid?" Moon-Face asked.

"Just fine and dandy," I said dryly.

We left the doorman behind and I let myself be herded between them until we reached the car. It was the same car I'd seen that afternoon, the car which had picked up Frenchy LaSeur. I got in. Moon-Face drove. Pug-Face sat behind me with his gun against the nape of my neck. The muzzle was cold with the dampness of the night and it made me shiver. I wasn't scared. That damned muzzle was just chilly.

Moon-Face headed the car southward down Central Park West. We rode for four or five blocks in complete silence. I didn't like that. It signified business and I wasn't in too hot a spot for business. I told you that you can bluff so far and then you've got to show the goods. I had plenty to bluff with, but nothing to back up my hand when it was called.

"Well, boys?" I said.

THEY WOULDN'T ANSWER me. Pug-Face rubbed my

neck with the Colt pistol significantly, but there were no words. The night was very damp. Somewhere west of us along the Hudson, a ship hooted dismally like a lonesome snow owl. Otherwise, the city seemed wrapped in a deathly calm. It wasn't really; cabs went by us, honking merrily. The Barbizon-Plaza glowed at the southern fringe of the Park. The Empire tower looked gay enough. Yet somehow, I began to feel cold, a ghostly chill permeating my bones.

I broke the ice again. "Well, boys?" I said.

The pistol nudged me but I shook my head, looking annoyed and I snapped: "Stop kidding with the rod, Wall-flower. You know you're not going to use it. Durken told you to take it easy. He's not killing the goose that lays the golden eggs and you and I know it."

"You talk smart." Pug-Face growled.

"Lay off, Halson," said Moon-Face. "Jones wasn't born yesterday. And he happens to be right."

"You couldn't bump me until Durken got his paws on those pictures I took," I said.

"Sure," said Moon-Face quietly. "Sure—that's it. But look, Candid. There's nothing in the books says we can't lay an egg on your skull with the barrel of that rod. An unconscious ex-dick is just as good as a live one. Maybe better in your case."

"I'm behaving," I said.

"And this was the hard-boiled shamus," said Pug-Face Halson. "This was the guy they usta tip their hats to. He don't look hard-boiled to me."

I laughed and nudged Moon-Face. "You—what's your name?"

"I'm Baccy Malone," said Moon-Face.

"You ought to tell you're friend that I don't think he looks even intelligent. He never bothered to frisk me."

Halson gasped. "It's a fact." And instantly his hands passed over my body.

"Sap," smiled Baccy Malone. "Think he'd remind you, if he had a heater on him? Lay off, Halson. He's way ahead of you."

"And you?" I asked.

Malone shrugged. "Maybe so. I believe the things I've heard about you. Willy-Nilly tells me you used to be miraculous and he's no slouch himself. The guy's afraid of you, so I'm no sucker. But it ain't up to me, Candid. It's up to Phil Durken. He's *not* afraid of you. He hates your guts after what you pulled tonight."

"So what happens to me?"

He shrugged again. "When he gets the pictures—" he snapped his fingers.

"But he isn't going to get the pictures," I said.

"Then what can he lose by putting the slug on you?"

"You've got something there."

No more was said. We reached Central Park South and they cut eastward. In a few minutes more we were on Fifth Avenue and they turned down it, riding at a slow comfortable speed as though they were in no hurry. I guessed that they were heading for the studio. "Uh-uh, boys," I said. "That's not the place to go. Did you ever hear of a guy named Rentano?"

"Rentano?" murmured Baccy Malone facetiously. "Seems to me he's an Inspector of the homicide bureau. Not a bad cop either."

"Uh-huh," I said. "Not a bad shot either. If you're going

to my studio, I don't mind letting you in on the secret. He's waiting there for me."

MALONE AND HALSON both laughed loudly. "Boy, you're slipping," Halson said gruffly. "That one is older 'n' the hills. Rentano waiting for you! Ha! Pal, nobody's waiting there for you but Willy-Nilly Baker. And he's gonna make a try for them pictures before you arrive to save us the trouble. Sit tight, big boy, sit tight."

I knew they wouldn't believe me so I kept still. We were at the studio in five more minutes. They parked the car on Fifth and then herded me into the doorway. We entered and went up the stairs to the second floor. We stopped in front of my door: TERRENCE JONES—*Commercial Photographs.*

"In," said Halson.

The door wouldn't be locked, I knew. Rentano would have arrived by then. I opened the door. The studio was dark. I said in an even voice: "Candid, Harry. I'm the one in the top-hat. Let's take them."

And we took them.

The second I'd spoken, Pug-Face Halson jammed his automatic warningly into the small of my back. It was a mistake which nearly cost him his life. When I felt the muzzle there above my right kidney, I gave him the works. It was a police trick, a simple little jigger that always worked.

When a gun was in your lower back, you could spin on a heel, one elbow held stiffly down, and you could revolve fast enough to knock the gun-mouth aside with your stiff elbow before a killer could react fast enough to pull the trigger and burn you. It was worked out scientifically and it couldn't miss, and your only trouble was to find the gun wrist after you had the rod out of your back. You had to hang onto the gun wrist then or you might be in for trouble.

I spun. My right elbow caught the side of his barrel neatly. It knocked the pistol off to the right of me. I grabbed down and got both my hands locked over the gun wrist and then I fell forward on my face as hard as I could. Halson's own weight tricked him.

He flew over my back and went high into the air. When he was up off his feet, I leaned on that arm of his and it did damn queer things. He shrieked. He was hurt badly from the sound of it. He dropped the gun. I picked it up and dove at him from my knees and I hit him on the chin with it twice, long sweeping blows.

Baccy Malone panicked, I guess. He fired once at my back and missed me. And then Inspector Rentano came to life.

I don't know what part of the darkened studio he was sitting in, and I didn't see the flash of his Police Positive .38, but I heard its stolid bark and I heard Baccy Malone's thud when he hit the floor and then I yelled: "Lights, Harry!" And the lights came on.

But Rentano didn't put them on. Rentano was sitting in my easy chair when I saw him, his face grim and his eyes like slits. And the guy who had turned on the lights was Detective Snagle of Rentano's h.q. detail. And what's more—Willy-Nilly Baker was lying on the floor with a pair of handcuffs on his wrists and his wrists behind his back.

"Are you all right, Candid?" Rentano asked.

"Elegant," I said. I got up and picked my top hat off the

floor and put it on my head. I dusted off my coat. Then I took a look at Pug-Face Halson.

HE LOOKED SICK. His face was all bloody and I could see from the peculiar twist of it that his right wing was all broken up from the midair turning. He was crying pellucid tears with the pain that ate him, crying out loud like a child.

"That's that," Rentano said. "I had Snagle tailing Willy-Nilly Baker and Durken. Durken met Frenchy LaSeur and they're at Jimmy LaVerne's White Slipper Club right now. So Snagle tailed Baker to see what was what and Baker came here. We caught him when he tried to bust up this place. He was after the pictures. You know."

"Sure," I said. "So were these boys. But why so grim?"

"Willy-Nilly's dead," said Rentano. "I hit him on the back of the head. Meant to konk him, but his skull caved. I wanted to take him alive. He would have talked."

Detective Snagle was bending over Baccy Malone. "You got this guy for keeps, Inspector. Dead."

"No," I said, a little shocked. I shouldn't have been, but in a way I was sorry. Baccy Malone had been a pretty normal guy for a hood. I couldn't help half-liking him."

"Yeah," said Rentano gloomily. "I was playing for keeps when I shot him. He had a gun on your back, Candid."

"Through the forehead," said Snagle. "Keeps is the word,"

There was a long silence. Then Rentano sighed. "That's me. Impetuous. I wanted Willy-Nilly to talk. And what've we got. A guy with a busted wing. And he'll talk all right and implicate himself and turn state's evidence, but what weight will that carry when we try to indict Frenchy and Durken. His word won't mean a thing there. He'll say we broke him up to get him to confess. And he looks like we did."

Another silence. Finally I said: "Look, Harry. There's one way to get Frenchy LaSeur."

"I know." Rentano looked very serious. "Shoot it out with him. I'd like it that way. I'd be sure."

Detective Snagle whistled and looked at the ceiling. "Pat McCoy was a white man, chief," he said. "I'll handle the job if you say so."

"It's my job," Rentano replied. "But who'll cover Durken when we catch up with them?"

"I will," I said.

"*You?*"

I went to my cabinet and unlocked it and I took out my Lüger and examined it. It was primed, oiled, loaded, ready to go. I weighed it carefully in my hand once, then slipped it into my coat. "A pleasure, Harry, a pleasure."

"But all along you've said—"

"Forget what I said. You told me I had cop in my blood. Well, you're right. It's not only Pat McCoy. It's the other white men like him. They go to make way for rats. Yellow, mangy rats who'd kill their own grandmothers for the right price. You were right when you said I couldn't stomach crime. I can't. And I can't stomach rats, either—crime or no crime."

"You mean," Rentano said happily, "you're in? You're in, Candid?"

I took a slow breath and smiled coldly. "Not in, Harry. Back. Back is the word. Back to stay. I'm a dick. I'll always be a dick. I'm going back to the gumshoe trail for keeps, Harry."

"Ye Gods!" breathed Rentano excitedly. "*Let's go!*"

5

YOU CAN'T KILL A COP

THE WHITE SLIPPER Club, on West 45th was one of the
smartest night spots on the gay white way. Jimmy LaVerne
ran it and he was a square gambler; he worked his charities
and he helped the police fund and his wheels were honest.
He was so square, every cop in town knew there were heels
behind the dance floor front of the club—and they all shut
their eyes to the fact, Rentano included.

By the time we reached the White Slipper it was near
midnight and the after-theater crowd had piled in until
there was just about standing-room. The people were all
in evening dress and most of them were either guzzling at
the resplendent mirror-lined bar or were dancing on the
floor while the orchestra played. We left Snagle to cover
the door in case anything broke wrong. And then Rentano
and I went inside.

I was in full dress so no one looked at me twice. But even
Rentano wasn't conspicuous in his business suit. Other
men were dressed similarly and when we found Durken
and Frenchy LaSeur, seated at a table on the edge of the
dance floor with a pair of blonde bimboes beside them, we
saw that they were both in street clothes too.

It was the first time I'd seen Frenchy LaSeur's face. And

the instant I saw it, I knew LaSeur would bust wide open under a little pressure. It was because he didn't have a chin and his black eyes wouldn't stay put in one place. Just that, and I tabbed him. I tabbed him for a snow-bird and a stooly and a squeeler and I told Rentano so.

Rentano stiffened when he saw LaSeur.

"Careful, Harry," I said. "You won't have to go all the way with him. Remember all the witnesses around here. You couldn't ask for anything else. He'll tumble. You can take him."

"I can take him," repeated Rentano grimly. "Hang on to Durken. He'll blast when the going gets hot."

"Let's go, then."

"Right. There goes Frenchy with the blonde for a dance. I'm stepping in. Cover me."

I eased over behind Phil Durken. In the crowd he never saw me and no one else noticed me. I saw Inspector Rentano go through the aisles.

Then Durken saw Rentano, and Durken tightened like a ramrod. He pushed his blonde aside and told her to shut up, his eyes boring into Rentano's back, his crooked cheek twitching nervously.

Rentano reached Frenchy LaSeur, jerked him around, pushed the girl away and said something to Frenchy. I couldn't hear it then, but Rentano told me later it was: "Call it a day, Frenchy. You're under arrest for the murder of Patrick McCoy."

And Frenchy had replied: "Nuts, Inspector. You've got nothing on me. I got an alibi. I told you—"

"Nuts to you," Rentano had replied in turn. "You didn't get Candid Jones, Frenchy. And Willy-Nilly didn't get those pictures. He's dead. And so is Baccy Malone. And Halson is in the cooler talking his head off. And those pictures Candid Jones took will fry your seat in the chair. Put out your hands!"

ALL THIS WENT on between them without anyone else hearing. After Rentano's last build-up, Frenchy LaSeur let out a shriek of terror. I heard that. So did the rest of the population of the White Slipper.

The dance floor cleared like magic, leaving Frenchy and Rentano alone there facing each other like two gladiators. There was a gun in Frenchy's hand that weaved back and forth.

Rentano spoke hollowly. "I call upon all of you as witnesses that this man drew first." But Rentano didn't need witnesses. I had the Leica out and in my hands. I opened the Summar lens to f/2 and took the picture at one-twenty-fifth of a second. It was a neat shot, because a spotlight was on the both of them. It showed Frenchy heeled with a rod—and Inspector Rentano unarmed. And then in a twinkling his Police Positive snapped out and trained on Frenchy's stomach.

That was too much for the rat. He quailed in the face of that ominous black muzzle, noted for its accuracy. He threw down his own gun and began to blubber and say things that were surely putting him in the electric chair. "Don't shoot! Inspector, don't shoot! I'll go—I'll talk! I did it—bumped Joe Kelsy—bumped Pat McCoy—I'll tell you how it was—"

Close to me, Phil Durken could see his name coming up in Frenchy's squealy confession as the mastermind behind the whole business. He could see that, and maybe with his imagination, he could see an electrocution, too. Very quietly he reached into a shoulder holster and brought out the .45 I had taken from him earlier that evening. He leveled it at Frenchy under the table, but he didn't press the trigger.

I sat down next to him, laid the Leica on the table and pressed the Lüger into the left side of him where his heart pumped.

"Slack that finger, Durken," I said. "We were to kill each other on sight, weren't we? Who wins, Durken, who wins?"

He knew it was me. He didn't have to turn and look. His eyes stayed on Frenchy and the sweat popped out on his face from the strain that moved throughout him and left his gun hand nervously caressing the Colt there.

"Who wins?" I asked quietly. "Kill Frenchy and I'll put one through your heart right where you sit. Don't kill Frenchy and he talks you into the chair. Who wins, Durken?"

It took a tremendous effort. He dropped the gun to the floor and then heaved a mournful weary sigh. "You win, Candid," he said. "You've taken me."

I said. "You can't kill a cop. Durken. You made a mistake when you killed Pat McCoy. Now talk. Talk quietly and easily and completely. And lay it on the line. Who is this Kelsy that Frenchy says he killed?"

"Hell," Durken spat.

"Talk."

"He was a cheap grafter. He got hold of some letters. They belonged to the show girl, Jane Rickert. He squeezed her and she got Pat McCoy to break the case for her. When Kelsey heard McCoy was on his trail, he blew his top.

Came to me and offered to give me the letters and split with me on what I got out of Jane Rickert. But before he could get the letters to me, McCoy reached him, got the letters first."

"Sure," I said. "So you had Kelsy bumped to cover the trail and you went after McCoy when he was delivering the letters to Jane Rickert. You killed him and took the letters and instantly started to squeeze the girl again."

"I didn't want McCoy bumped," he said. "Frenchy—he got nervous—"

"Give me those letters."

He took them out of his pocket. They were still in the manila envelope. I took a look at them. I had to read them in order to be sure they were the goods. They made my face burn. Jane Rickert had been a trifle indiscreet with a guy named Andre Marion.

Rentano came over with Frenchy. He was grinning from ear to ear. "Indictment?" Rentano said cheerfully. "No worry about that. We've got enough on these guys to keep 'em in storage until the next ice age. And witnesses— take a look at them. People whose word would count. And they've signed on the dotted line. Let's go." We went.

WE TOOK THOSE boys down to h.q. and the last I saw of them was in Rentano's office. "If you should beat this rap and come out alive," I told Durken, "you won't live long anyhow. That's a promise. So long."

"Hell," he spat crookedly.

"A funny thing," Rentano told me later on. "Remember that homicide Poppa Hanley and Daffy Dill were working on?"

"Yeah," I said.

"That was Kelsy, the first guy Frenchy killed," said Rentano. "Hanley was handling that angle and we never knew the two hooked up until we heard from the ballistic department that the slugs in Kelsy and McCoy matched. So you never know, eh?"

"You never know," I said.

And incidentally, I didn't have to keep my promise to Phil Durken because he didn't come out of that rap alive.

ONE HERRING—VERY RED

Those Miami jewel Crooks Were
Playing a Reckless Game—And
Candid Jones Was Their Pawn

1

THE WIRE FROM MIAMI

BARNEY DOYLE TAUGHT me how to be a shamus—fat old Barney with his flaccid stomach, his electric light eyes, and his rollicking, roaring laughter. Barney was a philosopher and he'd known my old man like a brother. When my old man died, Barney felt responsible for me.

I never told you how I came to sleuth for Apex Insurance Company because it was never necessary. But the past isn't always forgotten and sometimes it can reach out and wipe away the present and the future. It did this time, anyway.

My old man was a cop, an ordinary patrolman. He was shot and killed by a panicked tin-horn crook. That was a long time ago. But something happened to me then. I'd never planned to hit the racket like I did. I'd never even considered it.

But when my old man died, victim of a screwball's wild slug, I first realized that it was in me to hate. That bullet was a germ, and its progeny consumed me completely. Hate is a big thing when you don't know what to do about it. I didn't.

I hated every crook I ever heard or read about. I hated every killer or potential killer or suspected killer. I hated every con-man, every shyster, every tin-horn. I used to sit and read the paper about some crime, and I'd squirm there in mute rage and wish that I could meet the guy behind the crime, so that I could put a bullet in his gizzard. You've probably done it at one time or another. But it's bad business. And it doesn't get you anywhere.

So when I figured to go into police work for life, I avoided headquarters and that line of duty. Too much discipline there and too many rules for me. I wanted a free hand.

I got a job with a little private detective agency and I stayed with them for a year and learned a lot about the workings. Then Mel Abbott was killed. Abbott had been in charge of investigators at Apex. I knew that his men would be moved up the line and that there'd be a berth open. Apex was a big company. I wanted that berth badly, because it meant going after the big boys.

That's where Barney Doyle really taught me how to be a shamus. I went to him that night when I read about Mel Abbott. He owned and operated the White Stag, which was a white man's speakeasy and club on West 53rd Street. I told him I wanted that Apex job and that I didn't know how to get it, because I was unknown and didn't have a rep. Barney took me into his office and we both sat down. He lighted a cigar and I lighted a cigarette and we talked.

"Terry," he said, looking me over carefully and casually, "you look more like your old man every day. The same red hair. The same long nose. Faith, the same red freckles! Why, with them freckles alone, I'd hire you if *I* was up at Apex."

I smiled at him. "But you're not. Barney. And I want that berth badly."

"Sure," he said. He leaned back and took the cigar out of his mouth and shook his head. "Apex Insurance Company

"*This is my party, boys!*"

is one of the biggest in this country, Terry. You know that. Anything that's worth anything is insured by them. You know *that*."

"I know it all right," I said. "That's why I'm scared. I want the job and I'm afraid they'll turn me down."

"Aye," Barney said, nodding sagely. "You're afraid they'll turn you down, because you're afraid you're not a good enough detective for them, eh?"

"Perhaps," I said.

BARNEY TOOK A deep breath and then sighed. "Look, lad," he said slowly. "There's only one kind o' man can play this racket and keep blood off his shirt front. Your father wasn't that kind o' man. Your father was as honest as the day is long and he had a golden heart under his ribs that was too big for his body. He was a good man, Terry, but he was only an average cop. He died because he tried to give a rat a break."

I nodded nervously and put out my cigarette.

"I'll teach you how to be a *cop!*" Barney said then. "A real *cop,* I mean, Terry, and not an officer of the law. I'll show you how to get that job at Apex. I'll do it right here and now. I can tell you these things. But the doing o' them depends on you."

I said: "I'm listening, Barney."

"You've got to go up there tomorrow," he replied with infinite care, picking his words precisely, "and you've got to tell them that you're the kind o' shamus who can close a case in twenty-four hours. You've got to build yourself, lad, you've got to *make* yourself a reputation. You don't want color. That's bluff when it comes to a showdown. Your reputation has got to come from inside and it's got to stand for all your courage when you have to take a man."

"But, Barney—" I said.

"What's your name now?" he said, interrupting me. "It's Terrence Jones, a nice Irish name for a nice Irish lad. And what does it mean to a killer or a crook?" He held up his forefinger and his thumb together, making an empty circle. "Nothing, lad."

I didn't say anything. I watched him and waited for him to go on talking.

"Do you know how you make a reputation?" he asked. "You make it by saying you'll do one thing and then doing that thing. You make it by carrying the fight all the time, always being on the offensive. You make it by being honest with yourself, by speaking your mind frankly and candidly.

Candidly! There it is! That's the ticket! Terrence Jones means nothing, aye, but—*Candid Jones!* The shamus who's candid with his tongue and his fists and his gun and—most important—his mind! The man who does the things he says he'll do. Candid Jones." He shook his head and smiled wistfully. "I'd like to see *that* man, Candid Jones. The world needs him and his like…"

I felt funny then, as though I were flushed. "I know how you feel, Barney. But do you think I could be—"

"Na, lad," Barney said, scowling and shaking his head. "You couldn't be. You *are*. Give yourself a chance and you are! But watch for one thing, Terry. Your heart. You've got to feel when it should be soft; not often, you'll find. Mostly, it's got to be stone. It's got to be hard—like steel. You've got to be hard with it. You've got to have callouses on your knuckles before you're through, and you've got to have a gun hand that's steady and sure and nerveless.

"And above all, you've got to be smart: which means break your cases and stay alive."

He smiled dully. "Mel Abbott didn't die of heart disease today, Terry. There's only a berth at Apex because Abbott was murdered—that wasn't smart of Mel Abbott."

I got up. "Thanks, Barney. You know how much I appreciate your telling me all this. I promise you I'll do my best."

"I know you will, lad," Barney laughed, rising and gripping my hand and hitting my shoulder. "And so when I say good night to you tonight, I'll say: 'Good night, Mr. Candid Jones.'" And I went out.

THEY LAUGHED AT me when I was interviewed up at Apex the next day. The man who was in charge of the hiring was Grant McNeal, a tough, frost-bitten old hombre who'd once been a name on the old Bomb Squad before Inspector Harry Bentano's time.

McNeal was—and still is—the kind of a guy who made the ten steps from the door to his desk, the longest ten steps in the world. That morning when I went in, he caught my eye with all the coldness of a fish's, yet they glinted with a flashing zeal which a fish doesn't have.

He started to scare me down by talking first. You're a private dick, eh? Name's Jones. What've you done? What makes you think you'd stand the gaff up here. We want a man here who's built to bring back stolen property along with the man or woman who did the stealing. You're big and you've got brawn, yes, but there's nothing in this record of yours—"

"Listen, mister," I said evenly. "The name is Candid Jones. Candid any way you want to take it. I don't sit behind a desk and shoot off a lot of steam when I know I'm not going to get it back. And I don't promise early recoveries of stolen goods and missing heisters. My only promise is to break a case within twenty-four hours and I keep that promise."

McNeal didn't get mad. He roared laughing and slapped the desk and rang a buzzer to bring in one of his men. "Listen to this rooster crow, Barton," he said to the man. "One of those guys who brings 'em back alive within twenty-four hours! A superman. You know the kind. Can you fix him up with a little job?"

I must have looked earnest because Barton didn't laugh. He looked amused, but he looked sympathetic too. "You might give him the Merrivari case," he said.

"Done!" snapped McNeal. "All right, *Mister* Candid

Jones. I like your style if it *is* style. If it's hot air, I can get all that in a Turkish bath. You go with Barton here and he'll give you the details of this Merrivan mess. You break that before noon tomorrow—that's twenty-four hours—and the job is yours."

I went with Barton. Mrs. Merrivan had reported the theft of a ten grand necklace. She didn't know when it had been taken and she didn't know how. It was gone. The insurance people had been on her husband's neck and had been all over the maid for the job.

I got the dope and played a straight hunch. I saw Mrs. Merrivan and talked to her quietly for two hours. And when I left the place, I left with the necklace, a promise not to prosecute her, and a release from liability for Apex Insurance Company. She'd stolen her own necklace to collect the insurance. I forget why now, why she had to have the money. Gigolo maybe. I got the job at Apex.

All this happened a long time ago, back in the past before the Rialto knew me. All this happened before I married and became divorced, before I became interested in photography, before I quit Apex in 1932 to leave a crime world behind me forever and make a profitable business in photography. It happened before I came back, before my ex-wife was framed in a killing she never committed, before Inspector Harry Rentano, my best friend, and head of the homicide bureau, persuaded me that I had cop in my blood and would never get it out, and that I'd always be a dick whether I liked it or not.

He was right too. I decided to go back to sleuthing on my own—mixing it up with a candid camera which was often better than a gun for catching both killers and evidence.

But you know how I came back. I told you about that before.

I only tell you about the past now so that you can understand the present; so that you can understand how I felt the night I got a telegram from Florida which told me that Barney Doyle had been shot and was dying in the Hermitage Hospital, Miami.

You can understand why I took the first Eastern Air Lines ship out of Newark an hour later, my only baggage being a German 9mm. Lüger, a Model G Leica, and a toothbrush.

2

TWENTY-FOUR HOURS

IT'S QUITE A thing to get in an airplane and take off from a town named Newark at nine A.M. in the midst of a snowstorm that gives you a few qualms. It's quite another thing to set your feet down on tropical soil at the Municipal Airport of Miami, north a bit from Hialeah, exactly eight hours later, five P.M.

It was so thick when we roared out of Newark, I couldn't see the ground after we were twenty seconds in the air. The air was bumpy up there too. But we left the snow behind, when we went over Virginia. And when we reached Miami that afternoon, I was sweating.

The thing was intriguing: eight hours from snow to tropical surf. But I wasn't heading for the beach.

The guy who had sent the bad news to me was named Al Morrow. I didn't know him from Adam's apple, but I wired him back that I was on the way and I asked him to meet me.

Now about Barney Doyle: when prohibition went the way of silent motion pictures, Barney closed up shop in New York and opened a night club in Miami. "It's this way, lad," he told me when he made the change. "Down there, it's work only five months of the year—and the money is all sucker money and plenty of it. I ain't as young as I used to be, Candid, and I like the idea.

"Besides, there's Jim's niece, Sheila. I got her on my hands to raise since Jim died." Jim had been Barney's brother. "I think I'd have more time for taking care of her by making my money in the winter and spending it the rest of the year."

"It's a good trick," I told him, "if you can do it."

And he did.

I must have been an easy guy to spot in a crowd. There were fourteen of us on the Douglas plane, but Al Morrow nabbed me the minute I put my foot on the ground. "You're Candid Jones," he told me. He didn't wait for me to answer. He steered me under the canopy toward the administration building. He added: "I've got a crate here. Let's step on it."

I photographed him mentally as we walked along briskly. He was a gaunt guy, medium height and very thin so that he looked boney in his tan flannel suit. He had a yellowed Panama on his head. His face was chocolate brown from the Florida sun, and through the length of his left cheek, a long furrowed trench curved down to his chin. He walked jerkily. His hands were very nervous. He gnawed the right corner of his mouth.

The car was in the airport parking lot, a lot which looked like the state of Florida itself. You've got to realize that Florida is flatter than a pancake and that its interior from the central orange regions on down, is nothing but swamp and lowland. It's a state of crazy contrasts. Those beautiful beaches on the east. And then that screwy Lake Okeechobee northwest, a lake that absolutely blew out of its shallow basin in that hurricane several years ago.

Florida is a state of marvelous highways—with rattle-snake and moccasin-laden bogs and peats on all sides. The whole southern part is so flat you figure you can look across from the Atlantic Ocean to the Gulf of Mexico. That is, you figure you can—if the red smudge fires of the Ever-glades ever die down. It's a state of historical wonders—and yet it's the vortex of every tin-horn rat who's after winter sucker money.

Al Morrow's car was a Cadillac, light lavender in color and with gaudy yellow New York license plates. He nodded me toward it and realized for the first time that I didn't have baggage. "Quick trip, eh?" he said. "No bags at all?"

"I just brought necessities," I said.

"Necessities?" he said.

I said: "A toothbrush and a rod."

He nodded jerkily again and licked his lips. I climbed into the car and he went around the other side and climbed in behind the wheel. He spun the starter, the engine caught easily, and we rolled out of the field and headed south past Hialeah toward the city of Miami proper.

I STARED AT the rear vision mirror in front of me for a couple of seconds and then watched the road. It was pretty warm out, in contrast to the snowstorm I'd left behind me in the big town. The heat waves shimmered up from the macadam. I began to feel sticky.

Al Morrow didn't say anything. He stepped the crate up to sixty and held it there, nervously gnawing his mouth. Finally I said: "How's Barney and what happened to him?"

Morrow thought it out a long time before he answered me. I had another look in the rear vision mirror before he spoke. Then he said: "Barney's dying, Candid. He was pretty near the end when I left him an hour ago. He's got a slug in his liver. It's a wonder he lived this long."

I didn't say anything. I felt too rotten.

"He was shot last night," Morrow went on. "Near midnight. He only regained consciousness this morning and then he asked for you. He wanted to see you badly. He figured you were the only man to swing the thing."

I asked: "Swing what thing?"

"I can't tell you," Morrow said. "Barney wanted to tell you himself. That's why he sent for you."

"Who shot him?" I asked. "And why?"

"Can't say," Morrow replied. He was more nervous than ever, and it began to show in his driving.

I took a third look in the rear vision mirror and then I decided to let him have one where he wouldn't like it. "I wonder how much it has to do with the flatfoot who's tailing us."

"Flatfoot!" Morrow wheeled full around in his seat to look at the Ford roadster which had been trailing us all the way from the Municipal Airport. His face went green and his foot went down harder on the gas. The car shot ahead as Morrow turned back and leaned over the wheel, his lips bloodless.

"He followed us from the airport," I said. A little runt with a black mustache and a pair of ears that hung down to his neck. He was a flatfoot all right. He had that detached air I once cultivated myself.

We had hit the concrete highway into the city now, after we had passed the pike which led out over the 79th Street Causeway to Miami Beach in the east. Morrow didn't let up.

We hadn't driven very far when Morrow asked me curtly: "That gumshoe still on us?"

"Two hundred yards behind," I said. "But why try to lose him?"

"We've got to lose that guy!" Morrow snapped. "Barney was going to tell you. He wanted to tell you himself. But I figure I better tell you right now."

I nodded, looking in the rear vision mirror. "Shoot."

"Barney's own niece shot him," Morrow said, biting off the words as though they left a bad taste in his mouth. "Sheila Martin. I was there. I saw it. She didn't mean to do it. She was excited. She was going to try and do a Dutch after the way Barney had spoken to her and when Barney made a grab, he twisted the gun against his own liver and it went off."

I said coldly: "Keep talking."

"WHEN THE COPS got him to the hospital, Barney was still conscious and he said he'd shot himself while he was cleaning the rod. The story's got to stay that way. If Barney knocks off, sticking to the yarn, then his insurance is okay. But if that gumshoe breaks Sheila Martin down and makes her spill the truth—"

"Out the window goes the insurance," I said.

"That's it, that's it! And Barney don't want that!"

"Is that why you wired me this morning?" I asked.

"Barney asked me to. He said you were the only guy to swing the thing. He wanted you to take Sheila and get her out of town—get her back to New York and keep her there and stiffen her up. Keep her in hiding a few days so that she could tell a straight kind of story for the boys from the insurance company."

I didn't like it. It was crooked and it didn't sound like Barney. And I couldn't figure Sheila Martin, who'd been a sweet kid in pigtails when I'd last seen her, pulling a riot act like that. Still, if Barney had asked me to do it—

I said: "Why was Sheila doing a Dutch?"

Al Morrow shrugged and shook his head wearily. "Ah, it's a long story. The kid's a knockout now, you know. She was going with a fast crowd and she suddenly found herself going around with Gyppo Grady who turned out to be a smuggler. Naw—not dope. Men—Chinese. He was running them over from Cuba in a fast cruiser. Then Barney found out about the thing and he hit the ceiling. He called her down so hard, she got the rod outa his desk and tried to take a shot at herself. So Barney's dying."

"Look," I said. "Forget this flatfoot behind us. I can square him if I have to. You hit for the Hermitage Hospital right away. I want a look at Barney."

"Okay, if you say so, Candid," Morrow replied, still holding his foot on the gas peddle. "But don't talk to anyone there. There's bulls around and they may recognize and lamp the whole game."

"I'll be careful," I said.

The Hermitage Hospital was on the fringe of Miami, north of Biscayne Boulevard away from the noisiness of the city itself. The place overlooked the County Causeway and the Venetian Way, and the whole green-blue lagoon in which floated Palm and Hibiscus Islands. It was a nice spot because there was land and ocean as far as the eye could see. And far east, white hotels on Miami Beach stuck up their towers into the blue sky like sentinels on the ocean front beyond.

When Al Morrow stopped the Cadillac in front of the hospital, I got out. And before I went in, I was struck with the contrast of that quiet lagoon before me. From where I stood, speedboats could be seen churning up past Al Capone's place on one of the islands. There were some seaplanes moored there, props dead.

And on the other side of the causeway were the beautiful yachts, quietly riding at anchor.

"I want to see Barney Doyle," I said at the desk downstairs. "My name is Jones and I've flown all the way from New York to—"

The nurse was young and sharp and very plain. But her eyes got very soft when I spoke. She interrupted me: "—I'm so sorry, Mr. Jones."

"Sorry about what?" I asked.

"Mr. Doyle died at two o'clock this afternoon."

IT WAS A shock, like an icy needlespray shower after a very hot bath.

I don't know why. I should have expected it. The telegram had said so. Morrow had said so. Still, death itself put the period on the sentence, added that touch of finality which is irrevocable and which empties a guy of feeling and leaves his insides numb from a mental novocaine.

I didn't say anything. I played with my hat and bit my mouth and felt all splintery over my eyes as though my skull were glass and had just been shattered by a hammer. It seemed natural to let my head drop to avoid her look of sympathy.

And that's how I saw the newspaper on her desk.

It was a late edition of the Miami World-News. I wouldn't have noticed it particularly except that I saw

Barney's name in an ugly black streamer across the first page. Staring hard at it, I slipped my hat on my head.

"May I see that paper?"

"Go right ahead," said the nurse.

I picked it up and spread it out.

DOYLE DIES OF GUNMAN'S WOUND

NIGHT CLUB OWNER TRIED TO STOP $200,000 HOLDUP

Saw Killers Who Stole Meredith Necklace, But Never Regained Consciousness Long Enough to Identify Them

Barney Doyle, well-known night club owner, died this afternoon at the Hermitage Hospital of wounds received last night when he attempted to thwart a $200,000 gem robbery at his club, the Royal Swan, on Keechobee Road.

According to the police, Doyle surprised a gang in the act of robbing a private dining room in the club, where Mr. and Mrs. John Meredith were dining. Doyle turned to spread the alarm, and was shot in the back eight times. The thieves then fired at the Merediths, killing them both. They made a clean getaway with Mrs. Meredith's diamond necklace.

Although Doyle saw the bandits, he was never conscious after he reached the hospital. Before he lapsed into a coma, while still at the Royal Swan, it is believed that he spoke with his club manager, Al Morrow, and divulged the identity of the bandits. Morrow has been missing since the shooting last night. Police entertain grave fears for his life.

There was more of it. A good deal more of it. The entire paper was smeared with the crime: theories, people who saw parts of the chase, of the getaway, of Barney Doyle, a first-class obit, an editorial about police efficiency and— yes, there it was. I'd expected something like that. There was a story about Sheila Martin. She had gone into seclusion, prostrated with grief.

Words rumbled back through my mind across a vale of years that seemed infinite now. Hearty, earnest, sincere words, spoken by a guy with a heart of gold. Barney Doyle's words to a young punk named Terrence Jones who had wanted to be a detective and who didn't know how to go about it. Priceless words: "… *You've got to be the kind of shamus who can close a case in twenty-four hours.…*"

I dropped the paper back onto the nurse's desk and I said: "Thanks," and turned away, and started to leave.

It was six o'clock by the big clock on the wall of the hospital reception room.

3

A POOL OF BLOOD

THE ENGINE OF the Cadillac was purring smoothly.
Behind it at the curb stood the flatfoot's open Ford, gyrat-
ing as its four cylinder job kept wheezing. The flatfoot
was leaning on his wheel as though he were asleep. Al
Morrow was pacing to and fro in front of his own car, looking anxious and tugging at his Panama.

I stopped at the doors of the hospital and I slung the
Leica camera out from under my right shoulder and took
off the lens cap. There was plenty of bright light in the sky;
evening was holding off a long time on nights like this. The
sun was still ripe and Morrow still cast a distinct shadow
as he paced.

So I stopped the lens down to f/16. I sighted him
through the Leitz rangefinder and when I had him sharp,
I snapped the shutter at one-one hundredth of a second.
I knew I had the picture all right. I slid the camera back
under my coat.

When I came out, I came out fast. I didn't have to look
grim. I felt grim right down to my heels and the weight of
my Lüger against my ribs made my right hand itch for a
grip on the stock.

Al Morrow's mouth was wet with his own saliva. He

kept running his tongue back and forth across his mouth and his skin was olivy with pallidness beneath his Florida tan. "You took a hell of a long time!" he said, jittery.

"Let's wheel," I said. "How about that dick?"

Morrow glanced at the figure on the wheel in the Ford. "He won't follow us now," he said. "I konked him."

I didn't like that and it must have told in my face. "Not bump, not bump!" Morrow snapped. "I konked him—with a sap. I always carry a sap. I walked up to him and said hello and let him have it over the ear. He'll be out for an hour. Let's lam."

We got into the Caddy and in a second we were on our way downtown.

"Well?" Morrow asked.

"Barney's dead," I said. "Died this afternoon. There's nothing I can do around here. I liked that guy. I liked him too much to be this close to him with him—dead. I'm heading back for New York on the first plane."

"Did you see him?"

"I didn't want to see him. The reception nurse said he was dead. It was kind of a shock. That's why I took so long. I had to sit down a second and figure it out. I'm heading back to the big town. There's nothing to be done here. I want to get away from it."

Morrow nodded eagerly. "Sure, I know how you feel. I'd like to go along with you, matter of fact, but I'll have to handle the club until things get in shape. But how about Sheila?"

"Sheila?" I laughed harshly. "Hell with her. If it hadn't been for her blowing her top and trying a lot of fancy stuff with a gun—"

"Now wait a second, Candid," Morrow protested. "You can't do that. All right, she went screwy, but dames are that way. You can't blame her. Besides—she's Barney's niece. Why, she was like his own kid. He was nuts about her. You wouldn't leave her in a jam like this, would you? And Barney asked for you—he wanted you to get her out of it."

I didn't say anything for awhile because I didn't want to seem too eager. We rode along in silence for a minute or so and then I said: "Okay. I'll take care of the kid. What's the idea—me to take her back to New York with me and hide her out until she cools off a little and gets some sense again?"

"That's it," Morrow said, smiling. "There's an Eastern Air Lines plane at eight o'clock. You can both take that. 'Course, we've—" he paused and cleared his throat, "—she's been fixed up so she won't be recognized. Dyed her hair blonde and stuff like that."

"I haven't seen her since she was sixteen," I said.

"Yeah?" Morrow laughed. "You certainly won't recognize her in her getup then. But we can't take chances on anybody at the airport recognizing her."

IT WAS A dirty brown claptrap house wedged between two honky-tonk hotels of questionable reputation. The big Cadillac just didn't fit in with the scheme of things. Standing there in front of the place, it looked about as congruous as a four carat sparkler on a panhandler's finger.

"This is it," Al Morrow said. "Don't mind how it looks. That's why she's here. Not a nice place. They wouldn't look for her. Let's go in."

"Sure," I said.

"You understand, Candid, the kid's upset. And she hasn't seen you in a long time. If she acts strange, you know why."

"Don't worry about me," I said. "I'll play ball."

We went in. Morrow had a key. He unlocked the door, then locked it again when we were inside. We went upstairs, after we left our hats in the hall below. Morrow led me to a bedroom.

The girl was sitting on the bed. She looked up like a startled deer when we came in. She was tall and thin and her mouth was small and her nose chiseled finely. She looked unhealthily pallid, a white skin, faintly rouged. She had on a light gray suit and her eyes were reddish as though she had been crying. She was blonde.

I had to admit, the act was very neat.

"Hello, kid," I said, being no mean man of Thespia myself. "Long time no see."

"C-Candid…" she faltered. She got up, staring at me. Then she ran over and threw her arms around my neck and burst out crying. It was real stuff. It was good stuff. If I hadn't seen that newspaper and if I didn't know that you can't change an Irish pug nose like Sheila Martin had had into a beautiful straight job like this dame sported, I might have been taken by the staging—*if*, too, I hadn't wondered why a girl like Sheila, out in the Miami sun for the past four months, was as pale as a torch singer who only saw what the sun looked like in moving pictures.

"Oh, Candid—" she cried, "—what have I done, what have I done? Uncle Barney—it wasn't my fault! I didn't mean to—"

"Take it easy," I said, trying to be gentle. It was hard to be gentle then. I was thinking of the real Sheila Martin and Barney lying dead at Hermitage and it gave me an urge to throttle the simpering sparrow.

Then Al Morrow said. "I'll drop out and pick up a little chow for you, Candid. We'll start for the plane at seven-thirty. Get there ten of eight. Only a ten minute wait before you take off then. Okay?"

"Okay," I said. "If Sheila feels strong enough to go."

"I'll be all right," she replied, wiping her eyes.

AFTER MORROW HAD left in the Cadillac, I began to cough dryly and glanced around. "Any water hereabouts?" I asked. "I'm thirsty."

"There's milk in the kitchen," the girl said, watching me warily. "Water, too. Whichever you'd like."

"Thanks," I said. "I'll run down."

"I'll go," she said hurriedly.

"Wouldn't think of it, kid," I said. "You stay here. Take it easy. If you put a foot down those stairs, I'll spank you. I'll just get a glass of milk and bring it up. If you want one, I'll bring up two and we can talk over them."

"All—all right," she said. "But hurry right back. I'm afraid…."

She had a reason to be afraid. I found the milk in the ice box all right and I did a quick job of filling two glasses. Then I sat them in the hall and began to take a quick look around. There was nothing on the main floor I could see. Just ordinary rooms, dirty and furnished by somebody who didn't know the hideous red-plush era was over. The cellar door didn't have a lock on it. I skipped down the stairs and took a look. The place was upset. There were dark stains in the dirt floor of the place. They looked like blood deposits to me, but I couldn't tell just by looking at them that quickly. There were no hiding places around the cellar. I went up to the main floor again.

When I got there, I could hear the girl calling me. I called back: "Coming up, Sheila. Keep your shirt on, kid." Simultaneously, a car ground to a stop outside. I went to the window, had a look. It was the Cadillac. Al Morrow got out.

As a matter of fact, Al Morrow didn't get out at all. The man who called himself that name did. I dashed back into the hall and was about to pick up the glasses of milk when I saw a little pool of blood forming beneath the door of a closet which ran in under the staircase. I set down the glasses again and tried the door, but it was locked.

Morrow was at the door. There wasn't time to try my keys on the door. I picked a glass of milk and met him when he came in. He had *my* hat on. His own Panama sat in the hall where he had laid it when we arrived the first time.

He stared at me. "Hey," he said mildly. Then he looked at the milk. "Oh."

"You didn't bring the sandwiches," I said.

"Say, I couldn't," he said. "That flatfoot is on the trail again—"

"You're a liar," I said.

Morrow started, his face clouding into a mass of lines. He leaned forward very tensely and stared at my face and then he tried to smile.

"You're kidding," he said. "You're only kidding, Candid."

"No," I said. I reached into my shoulder holster on the left and lifted out the Lüger and flipped the safety off with my thumb, as I set down the glass of milk. "I'm not kidding, fella. Stand still."

4

DEATH ON FLAGLER STREET

THE SILENCE LASTED a thousand years. Up over us on the second floor, the girl's high heels beat out a tattoo on the floor as she paced back and forth nervously. In the kitchen, the water from a leaking spout made a noisy drip in the sink. Outside, the horns of passing cars sounded in Flagler Street. Morrow breathed heavily. But all these sounds rolled together made the silence. I was too used to them to hear them and my eyes watched Morrow's right hand to see what it would do.

That right hand stayed taut a long time; it didn't know whether to reach for a rod or not.

It finally relaxed. But I didn't. I said: "I don't know who you are, but you seem to know me. So get this: what you've heard is no double-talk. About me, I mean. The first funny pass you make and I'll drill you cold. I won't even give you a chance. I'm cold-blooded that way, understand?"

"Candid," Morrow said, the sweat beginning to bead on his brown forehead over his eyes, "you got to listen. You got this all wrong—"

"Friend," I said coldly, "I haven't got a thing wrong. If you're Al Morrow, I'm Napoleon."

"For Pete's sake—"

"Easy does it," I said. I leveled the Lüger on a line with his stomach. "You're going to talk. You're going to rave like an ex-senator. You're going to spill a lot of beans—or you're going to die. And if you think I'm kidding, then call me."

"I know you're not kidding now," he said. "But you—you don't understand...."

"Who are you?"

"But I'm Al Morrow—I told you I was Al—"

"Oh, no," I said. "You're not Al Morrow. And the dame upstairs isn't Sheila Martin either, guy. You were taking me for a long time, guy, until I got a glam at the newspaper at the hospital. And an Irish pug doesn't change into a Roman honker in ten years. You slipped there, friend. Sheila Martin is pug-nosed and you can't change that."

He didn't say anything. His eyes strayed to my hat where it lay beside the Panama. His eyes looked very fishy and his mouth was working overtime.

I walked over to him slowly and I slapped him hard across the face. He jerked and fell back; his face where I'd hit him got livid. The slap brought a tear into his right eye.

He looked scared and he froze. "Now listen—"

"You listen," I said. "I'm through stalling. Barney Doyle happened to be a friend of mine. A good friend. I guess you know that now. I figure I know why that dick was trailing you. I know a lot of things.

"I know that you got your hooks into the *real* Al Morrow sometime today. I know you put him in that cellar downstairs and you tortured the truth out of him—made him confess that he'd sent me a wire asking me to come down here.

"I know you bumped Al Morrow. I know you had

planned to make me take this dame upstairs to New York, palming her off on me as Sheila Martin so that I'd smuggle her into the big town as quietly as possible."

"You've got it all wrong."

"SURE," I SAID. "All wrong. You guys were taking a long shot on me—an awfully long shot at that. The gems were on the dame. I was to take her to New York. She was to unload the necklace at her favorite fence, get the cash, and then lam. Meanwhile, you guys would take it on the lam yourselves and meet up together at a rendezvous and wait for the dame with the dough. All this other stuff has been a herring—a great big ripe red herring—"

There was a taint of horror in "Morrow's" eyes now. I saw that I'd spiked the whole works right on the button.

"Let's get candid," I went on. "There's blood on the floor in front of that closet and there's a cold stiff inside the closet. Open up and let's have a look. I'm not asking you. I'm telling you. It'd be easier for me to take the key out of your pocket if you were flat on your back with a slug in your spleen."

"Don't shoot—I'll open up!"

"Who are you?"

"George Nerfo," he said. "Nerfo's my handle, but you don't know me. I never did anything to you."

"Except pass out a red herring," I snapped. "Open up!"

He shuffled past me warily, never lifting his eyes from the black mouth of the big Lüger. He was scared. He was too scared; I didn't like him that way, but it was my own fault. He was ready for panic and panic meant a shooting.

He slipped and grabbed the wall to keep from falling. He looked down, repugnance lining his tanned face, green now from its paling. He had skidded in a dead man's blood which seeped out from under the doorsill of the closet. It was dark and ugly and still liquid. It clung to his white shoes. He raised one of the shoes in a dumfounded way and gulped when he saw the hue of the sole.

"Open up," I repeated, motioning with the Lüger.

It was night outside now. No sun, no glitter on the white houses across the bay, no scintillating heat waves to dance upon the streets of Miami proper; only light-studded darkness and the faint breath of the cool Atlantic which reached inland from across Miami Beach six miles away.

The light of day had faded rapidly as it does in the tropics. One moment you are washed in an almost unreal twilight, filled with the soft exquisite touch of a Corot. Then you are standing in the black of deep night, a Wagnerian transition.

As Nerfo fumbled at the lock of the door with a key, his face standing out luminously in the dark hall from the paint of a street lamp outside the window of the front door, I felt disturbed. It was as though you had been living with a ticking clock all your life and suddenly you felt alone and found that the clock had stopped.

It was the click which had vanished; the click of high heeled pumps across a wooden floor, a floor without a rug. The steady nervous clicking of a woman walking a floor and waiting, knowing a losing game meant an electric chair and that a winning one meant more murder and plenty cash.

I took my eyes off Nerfo's back just long enough to throw a glance up the staircase.

NO ONE WAS on it, which was what I'd feared. I had

forgotten the dame upstairs and it was just possible she might've come down with a gun in her hand to do a little armed ambuscading. But there was no sign of her on the stairs. The second floor was pitch-black. There were no lights at all—no lights in the room where she had been.

"Unlocked," Nerfo muttered.

"Swing it open," I said.

"What's the use?" Nerfo asked. "You can't see anything. It's too dark in here. I'll talk all right. Sure, it's Morrow. Sure, he's dead. But I didn't kill him, Candid. And I didn't kill Barney Doyle. And I didn't heist that two hundred grand diamond neckhanger and I didn't put the slugs into Mr. and Mrs. John Meredith at Doyle's club last night."

"In fact," I said, "you were in Punxatawney, Pa., when it all took place, feeding lollypops to the ground hogs. Maybe you didn't do the killings, Nerfo, but you'll fry for them. Open the door. Maybe next time you won't keep such bad company."

He stifled a curse and wheeled to the door. He grabbed the knob, twisted it, and flung the door open.

The body fell slowly. It had been leaning against the closed door. Now it tottered for a moment, then fell with infinite deliberation, like a felled giant redwood picking its way through the sky for the ground.

Al Morrow would never be deader. His body made little sound when it hit. Just a hollow thud, hollow because there was no rug on the hall floor. Face-up, it reposed in a rect-angular patch of dead white light which filtered in from the street lamp and cut a modernistic spotlighted patch on the floor.

The reflected light made the corpse's face a shade whiter

and waxier than death itself had made it. The effect was startlingly macabre.

Even more macabre was the sight of the four little black flies. They perched on Morrow's dress shirt front, for the body was dressed in a Tuxedo. They were flies without wings—black bullet holes. Some of the blood from the wounds had soaked into the shirt front. But the starch was thick for the most part, and the stains were centered mostly around the buttons and the buttonholes.

I'd taken too long a look at Al Morrow's corpse. In the dark, George Nerfo's feet beat a tattoo along the hall, and he was gone into the kitchen, heading for the back door.

I skipped over the corpse and went after him. There were no outside lights in the back of the house and the kitchen was so thick with darkness, you could have cut it with a blade. I came through the hall door into the kitchen and Nerfo opened fire.

He must have been in a blind, frenzied panic to have missed me with those three shots. He had made the back door and he was opening it—from the sounds—when he heard me in the hall doorway and whirled around to take me.

He didn't take me though.

Three shots, three bright flashes which lit up the kitchen for brief duration, three splintered cracks where the slugs hit the wall to my right and over my head.

I TOOK A quick bead on the night, one foot above the fountain of three flashes, and I fired. The Lüger quivered, but it didn't seem to make much noise. The night, split, stepped aside to let George Nerfo take the slug.

I knew he had taken it because the crash of his body

against a closet of tin pans made a terrific racket in the kitchen. You don't topple slowly when you're hit by a 9 millimeter slug out of a Lüger—not unless you've taken it through the head. That way, the muzzle velocity is so great, it goes through the bone without knocking you down. But when you take the bullet in the body—or through the heart as Nerfo did—you fall with the bullet, fall because you've been hit by a hammer travelling faster than you can close an eye. You fall with it hard. One second you're on your feet. The next you're dead—on the floor, bruised from the power of the fall, dead from the bite of the bullet.

The smoke of gunfire was still in the kitchen. I caught the bitter taint of it and sneezed twice. I took out a cigarette and lighted it. I didn't blow out the match, but walked over to Nerfo and held the match down over him.

He was still holding the gun, even if his neck looked all bent around from the way his head had hit the pots and pans in the closet underneath the sink.

I dropped the match and stepped on it, and then ran back through the hall to the front staircase. I went up the stairs fast, knowing the dame would have heard the noise and would be taking it on the lam. But I was wrong. The dame had heard me talking to Nerfo long before he opened the closet.

That was plain.

The bedroom was absolutely empty. A window was wide open, its dirty curtains blowing in with the wind from the bay. The window was just over the roof of the porch at the side of the house. I crawled out. A trellis ladder went down to the ground. The dame had gone down to the ground with it.

That was n.g., I figured. I'd missed a point there.

But I felt pretty good just the same. I felt that the hunch I'd spilled to Nerfo about the workings of the whole thing was absolutely right. And so it was—except for one thing.

I was to learn later that the dame did *not* have the diamond necklace.

5

TWENTY-FOUR DIAMONDS

OUT IN FRONT of the house, my hat cocked back on my head and a cigarette nonchalantly perched in my mouth, I considered the mêlée in the clapboard house from a legal point of view and I decided that, since this was not New York where Inspector Harry Rentano would take my word for it, the situation could have been better.

It was plain that, since Nerfo had fired three shots and I had fired one, I hadn't murdered him. The police would see that if I got caught up in the net.

Still, the dame had gotten away clean, and there was no telling what might happen then. She would go to home base, certainly and see the head man and the other boys—for Nerfo had been an underling plainly—and the head man might make things uncomfortable for me.

It wasn't that I didn't want to report the fracas to the police. That would come later. But right now I didn't want to get held up for a lot of questions while a lot of investigation went on.

So I decided to protect myself and use the Leica camera on the scene and bring back pictures of Morrow dead, and of Nerfo, just as the Lüger bullet had lain him.

The trouble was: there were no lights worth anything in

the clapboard house and while the Leica can take pictures *if* they can be taken, it could not perform miracles by shooting shots in the dark.

Down Flagler Street, there was a movie theater, not more than half a block away. Next to it was a drug store with a window-display of all kinds of photographic equipment.

I walked down the block and went in the drugstore and got a clerk. I said: "I want half a dozen photoflash lamps and a reflector-holder."

"Sure," said the clerk. And he wrapped up a carton of the number one photoflashes along with a one buck speedgun to hold the bulbs and set them off. In case you don't know it, a photoflash is a bulb that you use once. You press the button, there is a blinding flash which lasts one-fiftieth of a second and that's all there is.

The idea is to stop down your lens to f/8 or f/11, use your bulb timing, open up the shutter, flash the bulb, close the shutter, and you have a good picture on the film. Stopping down your lens gives a sharp depth of field and makes a good negative for enlargement.

I paid for the equipment and went back to the clapboard house. I'd left the front door unlocked so I opened it and walked right in. I couldn't have been gone for more than twenty minutes at the most.

The first shock I got was when—in the light patch on the floor of the hall—I saw only wood.

The "Al Morrow" stiff was gone.

I put down the bulbs and reflectorholder and got out the pistol. I went right to the kitchen and struck a match. I felt as though I were sticking my neck on a piece of running rail with a crack express rumbling down on me, lighting a match and showing myself like that. But I had to take the risk.

George Nerfo's body was gone, too.

But the holes that he had made with the bullets of his gun weren't gone. I found them in the wall where I stood as I felt for them with my fingers. I loaded the reflector-holder with a photoflash, and took a shot of the wall from three feet, the closest I could come. After that, I dug out one of the slugs, badly twisted, and dropped it in my pocket.

I looked at my watch. It said: seven-forty.

I WENT OUT. In the street, I found a taxi cab. I hailed it and climbed in and gave the driver ten bucks. I said: "I've got to make the eight o'clock plane for New York. Start stepping. Municipal Airport, I think it is."

"We'll make it," the driver said. "Hang onto your teeth and don't open a window or you'll break an arm in the slipstream."

We went off in a cloud of Florida dust. We made the plane on time.

Over New Jersey we ran into dirty, wet weather. If you've ever been up in the air during a heavy rainstorm when the air gets as bumpy as a washboard and your stomach doesn't sit where it ought to sit, you know what I mean. The scud went flying by my window when we first hit the low pressure area, and after awhile there wasn't any scud at all. There wasn't anything but a world of misty snow. It was wet snow, and sometimes it was rain and hail and sleet. The big Douglas didn't like it much because there were too many pockets and too many gusts, but we went on through all right.

The fog had closed in on Newark, the co-pilot informed us, so we flew on to Floyd Bennett field in New York and they set the silver ship down there.

When I finally got out and stretched my legs, I looked at my watch and I saw we were over an hour late. It was almost five-thirty A.M.

The airlines company had a bus waiting for us at the field. Only six of the fourteen passengers took it. It had us in the city in thirty minutes more.

Six A.M. Twelve hours of the twenty-four gone. I'd made a promise to a ghost but I was going to try and keep it. Twelve hours to go. Twelve hours to snare three killers, a double-crossing dame, and a two hundred grand necklace.

Inspector Harry Rentano wouldn't be at the office, I knew, until seven o'clock. So after the bus reached New York, I went up to my studio and changed to a different suit of clothes. I unloaded my Leica in the dark room and developed the cartridge of film in a fine-grain solution. I had a couple of good negatives on the roll. I hung them up for a quick drying because I wanted enlargements in a hurry, and I turned the fan on them hard.

When they were dry, I had a look. I blew up George Nerfo's head to nine by twelve; I let the other negative rest. I didn't need it yet. When I finally left, wet print and all, it was a little after nine A.M.

Inspector Rentano was sitting behind his desk at head-quarters, talking with Captain Soho McLean who, when he saw me, grinned from ear to ear and extended his hand, saying: "Glory be to Noah in a cloudburst, if it ain't the Jones boy!"

"Hello, Soho," I said. "I haven't seen you since the night you jumped that screwball's gun up in my studio."

"You mean the night I apologized for my remarks about your ex-wife in that murder frame," Soho McLean said. "I'm glad to see you, lad."

"Hello, Harry," I said to Rentano.

"All I can say is," Rentano replied, "you get around this country in a hell of a hurry. I heard you were in Miami."

"I was," I said. I frowned and stared at him. "But I didn't tell anybody. How'd you know?"

RENTANO LAUGHED. "THE arm of the law is long— as a matter of fact, I heard it from Poppa Hanley. That cluck, Daffy Dill, was on an assignment to meet a celeb at Newark, and he made a few inquiries in a routine way on passengers, leaving and arriving. He saw your name. Happened to mention it to Hanley who told me. Your sins catch up with you, you see. But why cut the vacation short?"

"It was no vacation," I said. "I went down there to find who shot and killed Barney Doyle."

Instantly Rentano was jerked upright, and Soho McLean twisted around tensely. "On that necklace heist?" Rentano snapped. "You know it's been on every teletype in the country! I'd like to be down there, breaking that case. What'd you find?"

"Hold your horses," I said. "Take a look at this print. The guy said his name was Nerfo. George Nerfo. He's dead now. I had to kill him last night."

Rentano gasped, then looked at the print. "Nerfo all right," he grunted. "Damn slippery crook. Knew a slug would catch up with him someday, but didn't expect it would be from the Lüger. If—"

"*Wait* a second!" Soho McLean roared, staring at the print. "Are you telling us, lad, that Nerfo was one of the four mugs who snatched that Meredith necklace?"

"Exactly," I said.

"But if that's so," Soho roared on excitedly, "then the other three monkeys are Gunboat Lewis, the Twister, and Hanny Loke. They used to run with Georgie Nerfo all the time, pulling some time hot ice heists around this town. They're New York boys, Candid, every one of 'em. And the head man is Gunboat Lewis."

"Who's this Twister?" I asked.

"A little hood who likes to use steel. Got a rep for stabbing a guy and then twisting the knife while it's in the wound. His real moniker is Toni Moreno, but nobody knows him except as the Twister."

"How about a girl—" I started to say.

"—her name's Mollie Feron," said Soho McLean, interrupting, "and she's Gunboat Lewis's twist. I know 'em all."

Rentano grinned at me. "Soho used to head the racket squad. He has a punching acquaintance with every one of those boys."

"Let's see the pictures," I said. "I'll want to make notes."

We adjourned to the Rogue's Gallery, where we went through the books and got out pictures of each and every one of them. Gunboat Lewis was a flat-nosed ape with big ears, big mouth, and closely-set eyes. Mollie Feron was the same dame who had pulled the sandy on me in the clapboard house on Flagler Street in Miami. Hanny Loke was a bald little man with a sneer on his lips and no eyebrows.

And the Twister, alias Toni Moreno was dark, swarthy, and had a knife-scar, very white, over his left eye.

I stared and took a deep breath. "Hold everything. This Twister—I've seen him!"

"You've seen him?" Harry Rentano exclaimed.

"Where?" bellowed Soho McLean. "Where, by the saints?"

"On the plane. He sat forward, two behind the pilot. He was on the aeroplane that brought me up from Miami. He was in the same bus that brought me to town from Floyd Bennett Field!" I took another deep breath. "The Twister is in town. He tailed me. He was put on me in Miami after what happened in the house—and he—"

Rentano and McLean stared at me. "What are you talking about?" Rentano asked. "You're not making sense!"

"Wait a minute," I said. I was remembering. And I suddenly realized that I had it wrong. The important point was wrong. Or had been wrong. I knew it now. I had it now. "What am I talking about?" I burst out. "What am I talking about? I'll *show* you what I'm talking about! Two hundred grand worth of it! And right on my own brain all the time!"

I ripped my snap-brim fedora off my head and began to feel it feverishly. I was right. There they were. *Inside the outer hat band!* I ripped the band off. An inner band of oilskin had been sewn in under the hat band. I cut the stitches with Rentano's pen-knife on his desk. I tossed the hat aside and laid the oilskin on the desk and opened it.

Twenty-four perfect emerald cut diamonds, each placed beside the other so that there would be no bulkiness, rolled out of the oilskin onto the desk!

They were the most beautiful stones I'd ever seen, each graduating to a larger size until they reached the central stone—a twelve carat diamond which glistened like a young cake of ice.

Rentano couldn't speak. He was struck dumb by the awesome sight.

Soho McLean whispered: "Great Noah on an Ark!"

I said: "The Meredith necklace—Barney Doyle died for those stones."

And a new cold voice emanated in from the hall at the doorway of Inspector Rentano's office. A new cold voice which said: "And you'll die for 'em too, Jones, if you don't stick up your hands and stand back away from that desk! This is my party, boys!"

6

THE PHONEY

MIAMI NEVER HAD seemed further away than it had until that voice spoke. Fifteen hundred miles of land and river and air was between me and Miami. I'd half-forgotten the swaying palms along Biscayne Boulevard, the summery sun, the green waters of the lagoon, the blue waters of the bay, the Hermitage Hospital, and death in the afternoon.

Yet—in the doorway of Rentano's office—stood the spectre who could make it all come back and prove it was real and that it had all taken place and that I had killed a man.

The guy who had spoken was a little runt with a black mustache and a pair of ears that hung down to his neck. Sure—the little flatfoot who had followed Nerfo (posing then as Morrow) and me from the airport. The little runt whom Nerfo had struck on the skull with a blackjack outside the entrance to Hermitage Hospital.

Inspector Harry Rentano's eyes glittered like a snake's and before the flat foot could say "Don't," Rentano had whipped out his Police Positive and had covered the man. At the same time, Soho McLean shuffled slowly across the room toward the shamus, then quietly jumped the gun in that way of his which startles you, and wrenched the rod out of the flatfoot's hand.

"Now!" Soho McLean detonated, his grizzled mustache jumping up and down like a frog as his mouth moved. "Who the hell are you and what call you got busting in here waving a rod around?"

The flatfoot was paler and a little frantic. "Wait a second! You guys've got me wrong! I'm a dick. My name's Phil Menken and I sleuth for the Apex Insurance Company. I'm a Florida operative. I was on the Meredith necklace job!"

Rentano nodded. "Keep on talking, Menken."

"I saw Al Morrow yesterday morning," Menken rattled on, "and I gave him a few questions but he didn't know many answers. He said he hadn't seen any one of the killers—four of 'em—actually, but he heard one talk and he thought it was an egg named Gunboat Lewis. I left him then, after he told me he'd wired Candid Jones to come on down like Barney Doyle had said. Then Morrow disappeared. I couldn't find him. I figured he'd meet Jones at the plane—"

"But he didn't," I said.

"—and a guy named George Nerfo met Candid Jones instead. I followed them to the Hermitage Hospital and Nerfo konked me with a sap there and I lost the trail. I kept in touch with the airports and eight o'clock last night I learned that Candid Jones had left for New York. I figured he'd turned crooked, gone in with the gang, was transporting the necklace out of the heat which the cops had turned on in Miami."

"So you followed me?"

"No. I knew I'd catch up with you soon enough. I

followed Gunboat Lewis and Hanny Loke and when they caught the ten o'clock plane for New York, I caught it too. I don't know what happened to Georgie Nerfo—"

"I killed him," I said.

Menken gasped. "I thought you were in with them—"

I said: "Which was very smart. Very smart. I suppose you also thought Rentano and Captain McLean were in cahoots with me when we were looking over the swag— good work, that!—on the desk here. Is that true about Gunboat Lewis and Hanny Loke being in New York?"

"Yes," Menken said, his eyes glowing on the diamonds in front of Rentano on the desk.

"Keep your hooks off these, screwball," Soho McLean snapped. "Candid brought them in and Candid will collect on them. And by the beard of Moses, Apex could do a helluva lot better with her operatives."

HARRY RENTANO CAME around to me and said quietly: "Anything you say, Candid. I can see that you're planning something."

"I said: "I'm only thinking this: Nerfo planted those stones in my hat. As a blind, I was to take Mollie Feron to New York. The catch was: I was giving safe transport to the loot—of which Mollie would relieve me when I got here.

The Twister, plainly, was sent along to cover both of us.

"As you know, I came alone. But the Twister was already on the plane waiting—and he didn't know things had gone wrong and that Nerfo had been killed and Mollie Feron had lammed."

Rentano took a breath. "I get the rest. Mollie Feron reached Gunboat Lewis and Hanny Loke. They came back. When you left the house,.they cleaned out the bodies and put a tail on you. When they saw you had headed for New York as per schedule—*with the necklace in your hat*—they followed on the next plane."

"Yes." I lighted a cigarette and strolled to the window and looked down. "The idea is that I'm still bait, Harry. What more could we ask? Gunboat Lewis and Loke and the Twister will be laying for me to grab my hat and me and the stones. They're in town, waiting for the chance. They don't know that I know the stones were in the hat. They're still playing the long shot—hoping that they'll be able to grab the stones before I find them in the hat."

Rentano nodded. "What are you going to do?"

I smiled. "I'm going to let them grab me."

"Dangerous as a two-headed snake!" burst out Soho.

I shook my head to mean no. "Dangerous, maybe, like a two-inch firecracker held in the hand," I said. "But no more than that, Soho. Not with you right on my tail. Get it?"

Soho McLean's eyes sparkled happily and he tugged at his mustache. "*I'm* to cover you, Candid, lad?" he cried. "And by the webbed foot of a Long Island duck, what a pleasure that'll be!"

"Sure," said Inspector Harry Rentano. "And besides, I'll be along too, tailing *you*, Soho, to make sure. Matter of fact, I'm getting fat. A little fracas wouldn't hurt a bit. And besides—I knew Barney Doyle pretty well in the old days."

I said, surprised: "You did, Harry?"

"Yes," he said. "I can understand how impetuous you feel right now." He flipped his thumb over his back at Menken who was still standing there, gawping in the sight of the diamonds. "What about this egg?"

"That egg?" I said. "I'll show you." I went to the desk and sat down in Rentano's chair and I asked for an outside line. When I got it, I called the Apex Insurance Company. They answered promptly, and I said: "Chief of Investigation, please."

Another short pause, a click, and then: "Yes?"

"This is Candid Jones," I said. "Remember?"

"Cut out the kidding, Candid!" said the Chief. "Do I remember! The nerve of you! I not only remember, I sometimes pine away for you. Anytime you want a job back here, say the word. What's on your mind?"

"Two things," I said. "A necklace and a phoney. First, the Meredith necklace—"

"You get me that," the Chief said, "and I'll hand you five grand in cold cash."

"I've got it for you," I said. "And never mind the cold cash. I've got the necklace. I hope to have the boys who heisted it before six o'clock tonight."

"Great Scott, Candid—" the Chief burst out in insane ecstasy. "How could you—"

"The second thing is the phoney," I interrupted him. "Since when does Apex keep operatives in different cities around the U.S.A.?"

"We don't," said the Chief. "Works the same as when you were here. If a case blows open somewhere, we send down a staff to break it and get the stuff. I've got eight men in Miami on that Meredith necklace thing right now!"

"But," I said, "not one of them is named Phil Menken, eh?"

"MENKEN? HELL, NO!" the Chief exploded. "Not one of them is named Menken! Why? Because I had a guy named

Phil Menken on the staff for awhile and he suddenly figured he could make a better living blackmailing our clients and he went crooked and got canned!"

"That's all I wanted to know," I said, "I'll have the stones left here at h.q. and you can have your company pick them up and take them off my hands. And you'd better come yourself on the job, because I want a receipt. So long." I hung up.

There was a movement for the door. Menken, wild-eyed and haggard, dashed past Rentano and beat a tattoo on the rug as he put his head down and tried to lam. But Soho McLean reached out a big number twelve foot, caught one of Menken's flying heels, and smashed Menken headfirst into the outer hall. Still stunned by the fall, Menken was jerked to his feet and hoisted back inside Rentano's office where Soho gave him an open hand which knocked him smack into a chair and out of it again.

"Talk, bozo!" Soho McLean bristled. "And never mind the double-talk either!"

Menken had tears in his eyes and could hardly speak. "Ask him," he said, pointing to me. "He knows so damn' much."

Soho let him have another one. "Skip it," I said. "He hasn't anything to say. Just another red herring across the trail—a cheap chiseling tinhorn who was using the Law to try and get himself a slice of the Meredith necklace. Let's get going on bigger and better game. It's almost noon."

"Lead the way," said Harry Rentano. "We'll tail you. You don't even have to tell us where you're going."

"I'd rather," I said, smiling coldly. "Just in case. I'm heading for the studio right now. Keep your eyes open and play for keeps."

"For keeps," Rentano said, eyes glittery.

"By the snakes of St. Patrick—*yes!*" roared Soho McLean. "Let's be away to drive the serpents out of Ireland!"

7

SUBWAY MÊLÉE

I HAD TO give Gunboat Lewis credit. He may have looked a little like King Kong and he may not have had any brow at all, but he had good men and the heart to take a chance on a long shot that was worth one in a thousand chances of breaking true.

It had been a good idea to let me, an ex-dick with a good rep, carry the Meredith necklace away from Miami. All roads were being watched, all trains, all planes, every line of communication, and the chances were that Gunboat and his boys would never have got through *with* the necklace. It was too hot to carry. The only other thing was to let someone else carry it without knowing it.

They only thought of me because Morrow had mentioned wiring me earlier in the day. I could see them figuring what a neat setup it would be to have Candid Jones carry the hot ice through for them.

And it was.

The chances—as far as I was concerned—were small that I would have noticed the stones in my hatband before the hat disappeared from my person. Even then, I couldn't figure why the Twister hadn't made a try for it in the plane or after we reached New York. I could understand why

Gunboat had let me out of Miami—even after he found Nerfo dead from my bullet, and knew that I knew that the real Al Morrow was dead.

Those things didn't change the picture. I could *still* carry the diamonds through unknowingly.

Perhaps the Twister lost his nerve when it came to make a pass at the hat on the plane. We'll never know. He didn't live to say, one way or the other.

The Twister picked me up the moment I left headquarters. He tailed me rather openly, as though he were completely confident that he was all in the dark and that I had never heard of him. The funny part is: he stood out like a sore thumb.

There was snow on the streets of the city. Everybody walking them—except the Twister—had a dead white winter skin from lack of sun.

But the Twister was brown as a berry from his Miami tan and you could have spotted him at a Republican Convention.

I caught an I.R.T. subway express at Brooklyn Bridge and the Twister caught it with me. It was crowded and we were both pushed together. I gave him a slow casual stare, and he lost his nerve. He gave me a sickly smile and he said: "Hiyuh. Weren't you on the plane from Miami this morning?"

I said I had been.

"I thought I recognized you," he said, licking his lips. "I come in here and I says to myself that you was on that plane. Ain't it a coincidence meeting in a subway like this?"

I said: "That's what it is. A coincidence all right."

The subway made a terrific racket and it was hard to talk,

so we stopped. The Twister stood close to me. I'm damned if I liked him that close. I couldn't help thinking of the stiletto he was carrying. Then, on the platform of the car ahead, a face peered through the glass of the door. A big round face with a warrior's mustache, the gimlet eyes fixed on the Twister, watching his every move.

IT WAS CAPTAIN Soho McLean. I hadn't seen him following and I hadn't known he was that close. But I felt a lot better.

The subway express stopped at Fourteenth Street and some more people got on. I saw the Twister nod slowly back into the car. As the train started again, flanges squealing as we curved out of the station, I took a casual look inside the car myself.

There were so many different peoples, it was tough going, and I didn't make out anybody for a little while, until we had wheeled through the Twenty-third Street station at full speed.

Then I saw Hanny Loke. He was hanging on a strap a few steps inside the car at a spot where he was generally behind my back. He looked pretty anxious and he kept jerking his head back and forth, once to look at the Twister, then to look at somebody further back in the car than himself. When the subway hit the curve just before the Forty-second Street station, I was thrown to one side. I let myself go just enough to take a look down by the center doors of the car. I saw enough to make me feel a little chilly.

Gunboat Lewis, in the flesh, was standing down there, ready for anything. There was no mistaking his tanned gorilla face. I knew him instantly, even if I'd never seen him before in my life—in person.

Like a flash, the train whipped into Grand Central and began grinding to a noisy, bumpy stop. We all fell against each other, then straightened as the train finally halted. The platform door slid open.

I took a deep breath, ran my hand over the bump which was the Lüger, under my coat, and then started pushing for the doorway. This was it. No doubt about *it*. Hanny Loke was struggling to get off at the center door. Gunboat Lewis was already off. I glanced behind me. The Twister was following in my wake.

And all for an empty hat.

Nothing happened up to the turnstiles. I got through them safely. I started to walk for the staircase which led up into Grand Central proper.

I didn't reach the staircase.

Something hit me hard in the left shoulder.

I thought at first that the Twister had slammed his fist into my back. And I realized quickly that he never could have had that much force in his arm.

I didn't feel anything other than the blow for seconds. But the blow sent me down headlong to the floor. When I hit, I felt the pain—a terrific wrenching thrust which hit me hard from the heels to the brain. I tried to roll over and instinctively I pulled the Lüger pistol clear of its holster. Every movement seemed to take a thousand years. The pain in my back left a red dancing haze in front of my eyes.

I felt my hat torn from my head, Somewhere a dame let go a scream, high and sharp. The red haze cleared as the pain got worse, and though I felt myself getting quickly weaker, I could see clearly now and make my hands do what I wanted them to do.

I saw the Twister running. He was running like a bat out of hell for the tunnel which led under Grand Central toward the Times Square shuttle. He had run about twenty feet when I aimed the Lüger at him.

But I didn't fire.

CAPTAIN SOHO MCLEAN beat me to it. I never had seen Soho work with a gun and I had a few lessons from the venerable old copper. He blew the back of the Twister's head off with five shots which must have hit within an inch of each other. Five shots hitting a running man that close. It was shooting.

The Twister was slammed to the ground as though a girder had fallen on top of him, and he never stirred after he hit.

The subway terminal was suddenly transformed into a rioting mad-house. Women were screaming and fainting, and men were running wildly for cover, leaving the combatants wide open in the station.

When the Twister fell, my hat flew into the air and fell beside him.

Hanny Loke came out of the crowd, picked up that hat on the run. He loped along, half-bent, his head on a level with his knees almost, and his hand shot out and flipped up the hat as he went by. But even so, he was behind the eight-ball.

I'd seen him break from the crowd to start that run. I'd also seen Inspector Harry Rentano break with him and tear right along behind him. Rentano had his gun out but he was saving his slugs and he wanted Hanny Loke alive.

He was a little fat and he was lots heavier than Loke, but desire made Harry Rentano fleet. He caught up with

Loke as the latter turned into the shuttle tunnel. Rentano hit Loke with the barrel of his Police Positive.

He missed Loke's head the first time and caught him over the kidneys as the gun arched down. The blow made Loke stumble. Loke lost his stride, began to flounder. Harry Rentano didn't. He caught up again, and this time the muzzle of the gun slapped against Hanny Loke's crown and Hanny Loke never felt the bruises he got when he collapsed because he was out like a light before he hit.

I think Harry Rentano had the closest shave of his life then. For Gunboat Lewis had broken from the crowd behind him, when Rentano had been chasing Loke.

Gunboat Lewis didn't waste time trying to get the hat. He came out firing two guns, both Colt pistols. One a .45 and the other was a .32 and he was letting both of them go at Harry Rentano. The only thing that saved Rentano's life was the fact that Gunboat was scared and he was trying to use the rods like a tommygun, spraying the general vicinity to clear a path for himself.

Soho McLean might have helped except that he was running for me, yelling: "Are you all right, Candid lad? Glory be to God, but I'm a sorry, man, to have let this happen to you—"

I was lying on my stomach, gritting my teeth against the pain in my back and the Lüger was in my right hand. I raised it and aimed it, but my hand was shaking too much, so I steadied it with my left hand and drew a sharp bead on Gunboat Lewis' left side.

I fired.

AFTERWARDS WE FOUND that the bullet had penetrated his heart, both lungs, then ricocheted out his other side and oddly enough had hit my fallen hat beside Hanny Loke's prostrate form.

I wondered about it at the time because I saw the hat twitch slightly as Gunboat Lewis dove forward on his face dead.

Soho McLean was kneeling by my side then. I heard his words vaguely: "This'll hurt, Candid, grit your teeth and hang on because it'll hurt."

He did something to me and there was no pain at all. There was just sudden darkness and a fine tranquility.

I came back to consciousness in the ambulance. There was a young interne bending down over me. He was dark and swarthy and he looked enough like the dead Twister to mix me up for a bit. I commented noisily upon the illegitimacy of his ancestry. He laughed. And everything faded again.

When I awoke again, I was in King's Hospital on Warren Street and it was three o'clock P.M. by my watch, and I felt pretty good. My shoulder ached, but there wasn't any real pain, and I felt a hell of a lot stronger and could see everything clearly.

Harry Rentano was sitting beside me. At the foot of the bed Soho McLean was standing. There was a nurse there, homlier than a mud fence, but she had a nice smile. And the Chief from Apex was there, holding my hand and grinning. But my biggest surprise was to find Dr. Kerr Kyne, chief medical examiner of New York County, playing medico for me.

"How do you feel?" he asked, trying hard to be professional.

I said I felt pretty good and I asked what had happened

because it was all none too clear. I heard Rentano laugh quietly. And Soho McLean cried: "Forgive me, Candid, lad, 'twas my fault to let—"

"Cut it out, Soho," Rentano said. "It wasn't anybody's fault. How were you to know the Twister would pull that sort of thing right in the station?"

"What happened, Harry?" I asked again.

"The Twister got you in the right shoulder with a six-inch knife," Rentano said. "You passed out when Soho pulled it out of you. But you got Gunboat very nicely before you went bye-bye. That damn' Lüger makes a terrible hole in a man."

I asked: "The others—?"

"Twister's dead. Soho—"

"I remember. I saw that. Some shooting."

"Hanny Loke is in the hoosegow. He squawked like a parrot when we landed on him. He gave us the hideout and we got Mollie Feron cold. She's warming a cell at the Women's Prison. It was a pleasure to tell Miami we had a couple of eggs for extradition. The indictment is a cinch and the trial is rather unnecessary. They found the bodies of Morrow and George Nerfo in the bay down there. Bitten up some by barracuda. They'd been weighted and dropped."

"Did you get the diamonds?" I asked the Chief.

The Chief grinned. "I got the diamonds. Here's your receipt. You're a sucker, Candid. It's no fun going around like this without getting paid for it. You can stick to your commercial photography too, but you may as well come back and sleuth for us on special stuff and get paid for it. How about it?"

I didn't have to think that over. I had come to the same

conclusion myself. "You're on," I said. "Candid Jones is no longer an ex-gumshoe. Apex has just hired him."

And later on, while I was lying there alone, trying to get some sleep with my shoulder hurting a little more, I thought of Barney Doyle. And I was feverish enough to see him come in the room and smile at me and whisper: "Thanks, Candid. Thanks a lot...."

FLASH!

*Candid Jones and Daffy Dill Join Forces
for the First Time and Scoop the Nation
on a Million Dollar Kidnaping*

Hotel Lincoln
Ann Arbor, Michigan
April 1

Miss Dinah Mason
Movie Reviewer
The New York Chronicle
New York, New York

DINAH, YOU GORGEOUS thing!

The first thing you must not do when you get this letter is to tear it up. Don't gnash your pretty teeth away and for Pete's sake, take your gnarled hands out of your standing-on-end hair. I can explain everything. Well—almost everything.

In the first place, I didn't mean to stand you up. But when a guy is working for a slave-driver like the little elf on the south fringe of the Chronicle's city room, he has to put duty before pleasure. Here's what happened.

I was standing on the corner of Broadway and 44th Street near the Hideaway Club yesterday noon and I was waiting for you to show up and keep our luncheon date— you were only half an hour late—when who should come riding by in his sleek black prowl car but Lieutenant Poppa Hanley. In case you don't remember, Poppa is the homicide bureau's only claim to fame. He saw me standing there

*Machine Gun Savell came out on
Candid's side firing a Tommy gun*

twirling my thumbs to and fro and he pulled up at the curb
and called: "Hey, Daffy!"

I wiped the look of surprise off my cherubic young face
and dropped said look lightly to the pavement. Then I
walked over to the prowl car and shook his hand and said:
"Poppa, my fran. You get homelier with the passing days.
If those ears hang down any lower, you're going to wear
out the collar of your coat from the friction."

"Haven't seen you since the night we laid the banshee
on 72nd Street," Poppa said. He seemed to be suppress-
ing some sort of excitement. "I suppose you're waiting for
a street car."

I said: "As a matter of fact, I am attending that angelic
vision, that displayer of platinum-haired locks, that young
and pulchritudinous—"

"You mean you're waiting for Dinah Mason," Poppa
said, interrupting. Wasn't that nice of him?

"I am," I said.

He took out a cigar, bit off the end, and then he started chewing lustily on the stogie. You and I know that Poppa has never smoked in his life. So the instant I saw him start chawin', I figured that something big was on the make.

I said: "Why the overworked incisors, Poppa? Has Hanley got another homicide in this fair city of ours?"

Hanley stared at me a second or two, then grunted. He took the stogie out of his mouth with great care. "Daffy," he said sort of hollowly, "do you remember Al Temple?"

"The Dutchman?" I said. "Old Baron Temple, the Broadway killer?"

"The same," Poppa nodded.

I said: "How could I forget him, Poppa? He staged a two year reign of terror in this city back in the pre-repeal days. He was the biggest beer runner in town. He was the biggest slot machine racketeer before the vice squad put that business on the blinko. He was behind the April Fool's Day massacre of those Schorelli mobsters in the back of that Bronx garage in 1928. Six of 'em shot down by machine-gun, forty-eight bullets in their backs. I covered that yarn for the Chronicle.

"Sure, I remember that palooka, Poppa. Baron Temple, born crooked, lived crooked, will die crooked. A big burly black-haired plug-ugly with an indented nose and dead fish eyes. He had a split tooth in the front of his mouth and he always stuck a toothpick in there."

Poppa Hanley shook his head. "That's remembering, Daffy," he said. "Not bad."

I said, "Pretty good, eh?"

"No," he said, smirking. "Just not bad. Well, I may as well tell you and break your stony heart. We just had a flash at h.q. on the teletype. A gang of ginzos walked into Al Temple's home in Michigan no more than three hours ago and snatched Temple's own kid—a two year old girl! How do you like them berries? That's eating the biter bit. That's irony for you! Gangsters snatching a gangster's kid!"

I said, "What a yarn! And me in New York without a chance in the world of breaking it! You mean to say— Judas! I never knew Baron Temple was even married! The last I heard of him, the government finally caught him on his income tax returns and he did a year at Atlanta!"

"That's it," said Poppa. "A lot of people know very little about Baron Temple. All they ever heard of him was his booze-running and his killings and his year in stir. Listen, Daffy, the whole time that guy was running loose in this town, cleaning up a capital of five million dollars, he had a wife out in Ann Arbor, Michigan, along with a home he owned under the name of John Brown. When he got out of stir three years ago, he dropped out of sight and finally turned up at his home. He's been living there with his wife."

"Tough on a kid that young," I said. "Who snatched her?"

"Nobody knows," said Poppa Hanley. "The F.B.I. is covering it already; local police in Ann Arbor are up to their ears in it. Boy, I'd like to be out there! I've got hunches!"

"What kind of hunches?" I asked.

"Well, listen," said Hanley. "Remember the boys who used to be in Temple's mob? No, you don't, I can see that. I'll spill them off for you. There was Machine Gun Jimmy Savell. The little pint-size runt who never said a word. I've always sworn Temple had him do the job on the Schorelli boys in that garage. There was Pinky Sherman, who took care of collections. An effeminate sort of killer. Acted like a sissy but could throw lead from a .45 like Buffalo Bill. The only one in the mob who wasn't a rat. Pinky Sherman could take it standing. There was Black Benny Dorgan, who hated Temple's guts and wanted to be mob leader himself. A fat, smart guy. Very clever, like a snake. And very oily like a virgin gusher. I always wanted to pot Black Benny but I never got the chance. There was Rork Shapiro, the smiling killer. He could knock them off laughing from his stomach up. Some crew, eh?"

I said: "Yeah. What's your hunch?"

"After repeal, Temple broke up the mob. He was stepping out of the rackets. He did his time at Atlanta and figured he'd lead a life of ease on the five million fish, savvy?"

"Smart," I said.

"Yeah—but Black Benny Horgan thought he was smarter. He kept the boys together. I think they did a series of jewel heists around this burg, but we could never lay it on them. Big boys, Daffy, with a shyster who can work miracles with a habeas corpus writ... I have not seen Black Benny, nor Machine Gun Jimmy, nor Pinky Sherman, nor Rork Shapiro around New York for two months. I remember how Black Benny hated Al Temple. And so I figure those boys went west, laid a groundwork, cased Temple every day. And I figure now that they've snatched Temple's kid and they'll hold him up for a million bucks before they're through. They know he'll play ball. He knows they mean business.

That, Dinah my hollyhock, was more than I could stand. I said goodby to Poppa and I rushed for the nearest telephone to let the Old Man in on all this very elegant news. I called the Chronicle and got the Old Man and I started to tell him what I'd learned but I never got the chance.

"Daffy!" he yelled. "I've been combing town for you! Looking high and low! Listen now and get this straight. You grab a cab wherever you are and rip for Newark. There's a plane leaving for Detroit at two P.M. I've reserved a seat on it and I sent Solly Sampson down to the field with an expense account and a toothbrush for you. Grab the plane and when you get to Detroit I'll have another ship waiting there to fly you to Ann Arbor! You're covering the Al Temple snatch for the Chronicle and Kenyon says you can go the limit to get a top yarn! You'll find out about the details when you get out there. Put up at the Lincoln

Hotel and keep me informed by wire and telephone of any developments. And, Daffy, bring home the bacon or else—"

"Hey," I said, amazed at the Old Man's enthusiasm. "I can't go out there. I've got a date with Dinah for lunch at the Hideaway."

"Forget Dinah!" roared the Old Man. (He said it, Angel-eyes. It wasn't your very own Daffy.) "You get that plane pronto! Dinah's a newspaperwoman. She'll understand. Now lam!"

So what could I do?... I lammed. I met Sampson at Newark and I got my ticket and three hundred bucks and a Dr. West toothbrush from him and I got on the plane and before I could catch my breath, somebody said we were over Ohio. It's a marvelous age we're living in.

I haven't been out to see what's going on at the Temple menage yet. I figured I'd drop you this note first to make sure you're still not standing on 44th Street waiting for me. For while the Old Man was right when he said you were a newspaperwoman, I have my doubts as to whether you're going to understand.

Drop me a line at the hotel. I'll be here a week. Then back to your fair presence and that lunch at the Hideaway. This is hardly the place for my nine hundred and nine-ty-ninth proposal but consider yourself asked.

Hugs and hisses,
Daffy.

NA 55 DPR—MH NEW YORK NY 120P APR 1
DAFFY DILL
HOTEL LINCOLN
ANN ARBOR MICH UNIV STATION LISTEN YOU

SAWED OFF LOCUST PLAGUE STOP YOU'VE BEEN IN THAT TOWN FOR SEVEN HOURS AND NOT A PEEP OUT OF YOU STOP IN CASE YOU DON'T REMEMBER THERE'S BEEN A SNATCH STOP GIVE THE OLD MAN 21OP

NPR RPM—MH ANN ARBOR MICH 220P APR 1
THE OLD MAN
NEW YORK CHRONICLE
NEW YORK NY
WHAT A TOWN STOP NO LEADS NO CLUES NO NOTHING STOP WENT TO TEMPLE HOME AND GOT BOUNCED OUT ON MY EAR STOP WENT TO POLICE HEADQUARTERS AND GOT BOUNCED ON MY YOU KNOW WHAT STOP WENT TO FBI HEADQUARTERS AND GOT BOUNCED OUT ON MY HEAD STOP JUST A BOUNCING BABY THAT'S ME STOP LAY OFF ME UNTIL I'VE GOT SOMETHING OR I'LL PUT SPIKES IN YOUR SPINACH DAFFY 240P

Ann Arbor Evening Mail, April 1, 1937

KIDNAPERS DEMAND MILLION DOLLARS
Huge Ransom Asked For Return of Child,
Mail Reporter Learns
Exclusive! Copyright by the Evening Mail
One million dollars in cash was demanded today by kidnapers for the return of two-year old Edith Temple in a ransom note received by the child's father Al "Baron" Temple, Ed Browning, staff reporter, learned exclusively for the

Evening Mail.

The ransom note was composed of printed words clipped from newspapers and pasted together. Details of the note were not revealed to government agents or local and state police working on the case. So far authorities have been unable to find a single lead to the child's kidnapers.

NA55 RP—MH NEW YORK NY 755 A APR 2
DAFFY DILL
HOTEL LINCOLN
ANN ARBOR MICH
SCOOPED BY A HOME TOWN HICK STOP FIND YOUR NEXT JOB ON A WEEKLY THE OLD MAN 802A

Daffy Dill, Esq.	New York
Hotel Lincoln	April 2
Ann Arbor, Mich.	

LISTEN SCREWBALL:

About five P.M. on that day when you were supposed to have lunch with me, the street cleaning department picked me up and drove me three blocks in the covered wagon before they found out I was not a stray ash can. I couldn't blame them. I'd been standing on that corner waiting for you for four hours.

I must congratulate you on your splendid work out there in Michigan. I see by the papers today that some palooka named Ed Browning got a scoop by finding out the ransom note had arrived. I also read between the lines that another palooka named Daffy Dill was undoubtedly shaving himself with a broken razor while the whole thing was going on. May you cut your pretty throat.

You ask me to forgive and forget.

All right… I'll forget. As far as I am concerned from now on, you might as well be in a leprosarium. If I ever speak to you again, it will be only because my mind falters, and you shouldn't visit me in the asylum.

May you have a relapse,

Dinah.

(Radio Bulletin, Station WEAF New York, 8 P.M., April 2)

FLASH! LADIES AND gentlemen, we interrupt the Bide-a-Wee program this evening to bring you a special news bulletin through the courtesy of the Broadcast Press Service.

Flash! G-men of the Federal Bureau of Investigation had in custody tonight one of the kidnapers of little Edith Temple, who was snatched from her home on the afternoon of March 31st.

The man was identified as Rork Shapiro, known in New York as the Smiling Killer. He was formerly a member of Al Temple's gang during the prohibition era. It is believed now that Temple's former gang has turned on him and had engineered the entire kidnaping. The capture of Rork Shapiro was effected by a newspaperman and an insurance sleuth who turned him over to the Federal men. According to John Wilston, chief of the FBI, the two men were Daffy Dill of the New York *Chronicle,* and Candid Jones of the Apex Insurance Company.

We resume the Bide-a-Wee program now with Hall Flower's orchestra playing…

NA25 DPR—MH NEW YORK NY 1030P APR 2

DAFFY DILL
HOTEL LINCOLN
ANN ARBOR MICH
YE GODS AND LITTLE FISHES STOP ARE YOU
WORKING FOR ME OR FOR THE BROADCAST
PRESS SERVICE AND THE FBI STOP WHERE IS
THE STORY STOP YOU'RE THE WORST NEWS-
PAPERMAN IN THE WORLD THE OLD MAN
1034P

NA44 FGD—GH ANN ARBOR MICH 1045P APR 2
CITY EDITOR
NEW YORK CHRONICLE
NEW YORK NY
STORY BROKE TOO LATE FOR FINAL SPORTS
EXTRA STOP IT'LL KEEP STOP COMPLETE
NITE WIRE EXCLUSIVE FOLLOWS STOP
FLYING OUT OF HERE TONIGHT FOR EL PASO
TEXAS REACH ME AT THE GUNNYSON HOTEL
THERE FROM NOW UNTIL FURTHER NOTICE
DAFFY 1056P

HELLO? LISTEN, CENTRAL, my fine-feathered little friend, you voice with the smile, you! I want to call Lieutenant William Hanley of the homicide bureau in New York City. No... it's a person to person call... Sure, I'll pay for it... Who's calling him? Why, I am, of course! My name—oh. Daffy Dill... No. Daffy Dill. Daffy. D as in dither—that's right...

Hello... Is that you, Poppa? This is Daffy. My, my, what a nice telephone voice you have. You ought to be on the radio. You sound as though you were in the next room. Isn't this a marvelous age we're living in… All right, all right, keep your shirt on, Poppa. I just wanted to tell you your hunch was right. Black Benny Dorgan has engineered this whole snatch.

Eh… Oh. You heard it on the radio. Well, Rork Shapiro didn't say so. He wouldn't say that. But it's as plain as your face that Black Benny and Pinky Sherman and Machine Gun Jimmy Savell have got the Temple kid. They're holding up the Baron for a million bucks and they'll bump that kid in the bargain. I don't figure they'll ever try to get her back. They've got to cover their trail. They left Rork Shapiro in town to collect the mazuma while they lammed for the hideout. Now that Shapiro's been caught, no telling what they'll do. Might get panicky, bump the kid, and take a powder. We're going after them tonight… Who… *We.* Me and Candid Jones. Sure, he's here. Read all about it in the Chronicle tomorrow.

Now here's what I called you about. We got Rork to talk a little and he said Black Benny had a hideout near El Paso, Texas. But Rork Shapiro didn't know where it was himself. I figured you knew that Temple gang in the old days as well as anybody did. And that you might have a lead as to where the El Paso hideout might be. Do you know?

You don't… What did you say?… Oh! You *can* find out! Are you sure?… Swell, Poppa, I could kiss your hanging ears! Now get this: Candid and I are taking a plane out of here tonight for Texas. We'll put up at the Gunnyson there. But you find out where the hideout is and put it on the police teletype and I'll pick it up at El Paso h.q.…. You got that?

Thanks, Poppa, you great big handsome man! My only

regret is that you aren't along to lay one of 'em on the nose... And listen, if you see Dinah, put in a good word for me. She says she'll never speak to me again... What... Your wife said that to you once... And now you have three kids... Poppa! Such a thing to say! Good night, pal, and take it easy...

City Editor   Hotel Lincoln
The Chronicle   Ann Arbor, Mich.
New York, N.Y.   April 2

DEAR RASPUTIN:

Well, you've got your story by this time. I just finished banging it out right here in the hotel room and I'm in a hurry, so pardon the errors. I just called Poppa Hanley for some info, and things look rosy. So here's what happened since I got to this collitch burg, which is a nice town by the way.

I had a lot of hard luck at first. I went out to the Temple home which was on Ann Arbor road north. It was a modest little dive that cost around fifteen grand. Just a quiet place, which surprised me, knowing how Al Temple went in for luxury when he was in the big city.

I tried to get in but there were police all over the place. Finally I sneaked in the back door and I stood around among a lot of brass hats and cops and tried to look like a gum-heel. But who—of *all* people—should recognize me but Baron Temple himself. He hadn't changed much. He still looks like the good old gorilla he was and he still has killer's eyes. There's nothing more he'd like to do at the moment, I'll bet, than have tea for two with Black Benny Dorgan.

Anyway, I was standing there when Temple got up and came over and hit me one on the jaw. I am proud to say I remained on my feet and let him have one back in the bread basket which I saw was big and soft. He woofed and then started cursing. "That guy's a newspaperman!" he yelled. "His name's Daffy Dill and he works on a New York sheet and I'm damned if I have to have reporters in my house!" The brass hats agreed with him.

When I picked myself up off the sidewalk, a guy with a fedora hat stuck on the back of his head like a collitch kid came up to me. At that point, I almost didn't give a damn whether Al Temple got his kid back or not. But I'd seen her picture inside and she really is a cute youngster, chief, tiny and blond and pretty.

The guy in the fedora introduced himself. "My name's Browning," he said. "Ed Browning. Ann Arbor Evening Mail. You're Daffy Dill. I've heard of you."

"Glad to know you," I said, figuring we'd be friends. "How does a guy go about getting the news in this burg?"

"He doesn't," Browning said, sneering a little. "I'm the only guy who gets news in this town. I've got ins. Nobody else has. And that goes for you. Oh—I might tip you off to a couple of things now and then. Stick around."

Boy, was he hot! He was laying for me because I was the city slicker. And he rubbed it in.

I finally left him and went down to police h.q. to see what I could see. They threw me out there too.

After that I went to FBI headquarters and got nothing. I felt pretty low. So I went back to the hotel.

When I unlocked my room and went in, there was a man in my room. He a pretty big fellow, kind of homely, his face filled with freckles, his hair shiny as bright copper. He looked pretty familiar but I couldn't place him for a moment. He had a candid camera—one of those Leicas—in his lap and he was toying with it when I spotted him. He saw me and he slipped the camera inside his coat on a strap and then he got up. He had a strong jaw and clean eyes and I couldn't help liking the bird before he'd spoken. There was an air about him that meant Business with a capital B.

"You're Daffy Dill," he said quietly. "I've seen you before at the homicide bureau. But you don't know me. You pal around with Poppa Hanley. I pal around with Inspector Harry Rentano. My name is Jones. Candid Jones."

"Candid Jones!" I said, surprised and pleased. "Well, shut my mouth. It's a pleasure." And we shook hands. "What are you doing out here?"

"I'm a working man again," he said. "Back on the flatfoot trail. I haven't given up photography, but I'm doing special jobs as an Apex operative when they ask me. Apex Insurance Company had Edith Temple insured for fifty grand. They sent me out to protect themselves—get the kid back if possible. I suppose you're covering for the Chronicle."

"I'm supposed to be," I said. "But this isn't much of a town for covering anything but your own fair form with a blanket."

"I know," he said. "It's a closed shop. Have you got any ideas on this thing at all?"

I said: "Poppa Hanley figured that Temple's former gang had double-crossed him and had pulled the snatch."

He said: "Poppa Hanley happened to be right. Rork Shapiro is in town. But the others aren't."

I asked him if he were sure.

"Sure?" he said. "Look, Dizzy, I don't go off half-cocked like you do—"

"—such compliments!"

He grinned. "You can take it, eh? O.K. I know Rork Shapiro is in town. I got a picture of him yesterday. I had it developed. Take a look."

It was Rork Shapiro all right. He was just coming out of a dive and he was—as usual—smiling. "I got that from across the street," Candid said. "I used a two-inch tele-scopic lens. Makes a nice closeup, eh?"

"Candid," I said, "you warm the cockles of my foolish heart. But may I ask why you have paid me this visit?"

"Sure," Candid said. "I figured we ought to work together, Dizzy. You get the story. I'll take the pictures. And the both of us to take Black Benny Dorgan sooner or later."

"You're on," I said. We shook hands again and I began to like the cuss better and better. He had an iron grip and a slow smile.

"All right," I said. "You've got a lead. Maybe I have one. Follow me, my fran, and we shall see what we shall see."

We covered the dive and about eight o'clock Rork Shap-iro came along to go in. We stepped out on either side of him. He was lightning fast. He went for a heater and I started to grab at his hand. At the same time, Candid Jones konked him one on the skull with a sap and then we herded him into a hired car. He was out for half an hour. Shapiro was. Candid plays for keeps.

We drove out to the home of a friend of Candid, Profes-sor Wilbert Fotheringay. There we revived Rork Shapiro with some ice water. He came out of it with his same fixed smile.

"As I live and breathe," he sneered, "if it ain't Daffy Dill and Candid Jones! A lousy scribe and a would-be flatfoot. Still trying to make a living, eh, boys? Well, you ain't got nothing on me and you're going to pay through the nose for pulling this little job. In case you don't know it, guys, abduction is a criminal offense."

"You ought to know," I said. "You've done it often enough."

"Funny guy," said Shapiro, smiling coldly.

"Sure," said Candid Jones. "Daffy is a very funny guy and I don't like the way you said that." He let Shapiro have a flat open hand smack across the cheek. "Now suppose you start to talk, rat. Let's hear you spill the beans. You were in on that snatch, Rork."

"You're a liar," Shapiro said, trying to smile again and not doing so good because of Candid's slap.

"You're a liar," Candid said. "And here's the man to prove it. Meet Professor Wilbert Fotheringay."

"Why, I was out in the garden cutting violets when it all happened," said Shapiro.

"I know how we can make him tell the truth," said Fotheringay, stroking his white goatee.

"How?"

"By my lie detector," said Fotheringay. "It works excellently. I invented the machine all by myself out here during the winter nights. It's very ingenious."

He brought out the lie detector. It came in many parts. Fotheringay wrapped a bulb around Rork Shapiro's arm. Next, Fotheringay set up a motion picture screen at the other end of the room. Back by us, he plugged in a motion picture projector equipped to take a roll of transparent white paper which came off another roll affixed to the high blood pressure machine.

"Here is the *modus operandi*," Fotheringay explained at length. "The pressure bulb is fixed on the subject. Should the subject attempt to tell a lie, the pressure of his blood will jump alarmingly. In the manner in which an earthquake rocks a seismograph, that jump in pressure will make this pen jerk. This pen is registering the pressure in ink on the roll of paper. I turn on the projector and we see these bumpy lines enlarged on the screen and moving all the time. If Shapiro tells a lie, you will note an abrupt mountainous peak appear in place of the even bumps. You may begin, sirs."

He turned on the projector and we could see the pen line on the transparent paper transmitted to the silver screen at the other end of the room. The line kept moving steadily on and off the screen as it registered Shapiro's blood pressure.

Shapiro tried to break away but I held him. His eyes were furtive and a little frightened. He didn't like the lie detector. Candid Jones took out a pistol. It was a terrifically big cannon, a Lüger. Instinctively, I edged away from it. Shapiro's eyes popped when he saw it. Candid said: "You handle the questions, Daffy. I'll handle the slugs in case Rork blows his top."

I stood up and shook a finger in Shapiro's face. "You were in on the Temple snatch, Rork," I said evenly.

"No, damn it!" Shapiro shouted. "I wasn't! I didn't have anything to do with it!"

We looked at the screen. It looked as though the Rocky Mountains had just moved in on the flatness of the Arabian desert.

Fotheringay said: "Oh, how he lied! Oh, I never saw the machine register lies with such verve as this time!"

"The truth," said Candid Jones. "You can't beat a machine, Rork. It's got the finger on you and you'd better play ball."

Rork Shapiro was panting. It was beginning to get him and you couldn't blame him very much. He pleaded, "Listen boys, you've got me all wrong. Give me a break. I'm clean on this—"

The lie detector registered Pike's Peak. Fotheringay said, "Oh, he's still lying, gentlemen. He's still lying."

I said: "You'd better come clean, Rork. You can't beat that machine. You were in on that snatch, weren't you?"

"Yes!" he shouted. "For Pete's sake yes! Now leave me alone! That damn thing will drive me nuts!"

"And the rest of the gang consists of Black Benny, Pinky, Machine Gun Jimmy Savell?"

"Yes—yes—"

"He's telling the truth now," Candid said, standing in front of Shapiro so that he could not see the screen. "Keep talking, Rork. Where've they gone?"

"I don't know," said Shapiro. "I don't know—"

"A lie," said Fotheringay. He sounded very blithe.

"Where've they gone?" Candid asked, his voice steely.

"—El Paso—Texas—" Shapiro faltered, his eyes rolling a little and his face as white as death. "Benny's got a hideout there—I don't know where the hideout is—I swear that's the truth—I don't know where it is—"

"That does it," I said. "I can find out where the hideout is myself."

Candid Jones said: "O.K. then. Let's turn this rat over to

the G-men. They make guys talk even without lie detectors."

So we left and went back to Ann Arbor and turned Shapiro over to the federal agents. And afterwards I told Candid that Professor Fotheringay's lie detector was a wonderful thing but Candid only laughed. "Why, Daffy," he said, "that damn lie detector wasn't worth the powder to blow it to hell. Every time Shapiro said a word, his blood pressure registered a mountain on the screen. Even when he was telling the truth! That's why I stood in front of him so that he could not see the screen. Fotheringay is a nice enough old coot but when it comes to inventions, he's terrifically terrible."

So that's how it was. Candid and I are flying down to Texas at 1 A.M.—a mere—bare hour. Reach me at the Gunnyson hereafter. And for Pete's sake, try and make Dinah understand that I am, after all, just a nice guy trying to get along.

May you avoid banana peels,
Daffy.

(Radio Bulletin: Station KDX El Paso, 9 A.M. April 3.)
GOOD MORNING, LADIES and gentlemen. Your Renno—R-e-n-n-o—reporter is on the air with the news of the world. Ann Arbor, Michigan. Rork Shapiro, one of the members of the Black Benny Dorgan gang which snatched the daughter of Al Temple, former rum-runner and public enemy, was shot and killed by government men last night when he attempted to make a getaway while being transferred from FBI headquarters to a local jail. At the same time it was learned that his amateur captors, Daffy Dill, a

newspaper reporter, and Candid Jones, an insurance sleuth, had arrived in El Paso via the crack airliner Sky Queen, hot on the trail of the others in the gang. G-men also are on the way to that city and local police have been warned that Black Benny Dorgan is hiding out near there. There has been a break in the Temple case. No ransom will be paid. John Wilston, chief of the FBI, promises the apprehension of the kidnapers within twenty-four hours… Borne, Italy. Mussolini today announced—

NA33 RH—TRY NEW YORK NY 923A APR 3
DAFFY DILL
HOTEL GUNNYSON
EL PASO TEX
OH BOY OH BOY OH BOY STOP YOU'RE GOING GOOD STOP DON'T GET YOURSELF KILLED NOW AND SPOIL EVERYTHING STOP GET THEM DAFFY AND YOU GET A BONUS AND THAT GOES FOR YOUR FRIEND JONES THE OLD MAN 934A

NA34 RH—TRY NEW YORK NY 923A APR 3
DAFFY DILL
HOTEL GUNNYSON
EL PASO TEX
TELL YOUR FRIENDS TO STOP PERSUADING ME THAT YOU'RE A GREAT GUY STOP I WOULDN'T MARRY YOU IF YOU WERE THE FIRST MAN ON EARTH STOP IF I NEVER SEE YOU AGAIN IT'LL BE TOO SOON STOP ADD ANY REMARKS YOU CAN THINK OF IN A SIMI-

LAR VEIN STOP PLEASE TAKE CARE OF YOUR-
SELF MANIAC STOP IT'S NOT THAT I CARE
STOP WHAT WOULD YOUR MOUSE DO WITH-
OUT YOU DINAH 935A

(Police Teletype Message: New York to El Paso)
… FOR INFORMATION OF EL PASO POLICE…
DAFFY DILL NEWSPAPER REPORTER DUE IN
EL PASO BY NOW… HEREWITH MESSAGE FOR
HIM AND YOU… BLACK BENNY DORGAN'S
HIDEOUT NEAR EL PASO AS FOLLOWS…
LARGE GRAY FARM HOUSE ON TUELTICAPI
ROAD NEAR NEW MEXICO BORDER AND LAS
VEGAS… DORGAN PROBABLY THERE NOW
WITH PINKY SHERMAN AND MACHINE GUN
JIMMY SAVELL… ALSO KIDNAPPED CHILD…
APPROACH WITH CAUTION… THESE MEN
ARE HEAVILY ARMED AND WILL SHOOT TO
KILL… LT HANLEY NY HM SQ…

"HELLO? HELLO, OPERATOR. Please connect me with
Room 413 and make it snappy…Hello? Is that you,
Candid?…This is Daffy. I'm so hopping mad I could eat a
cactus plant and wash it down with hydrochloric acid!…
What's the matter? We've been taken, that's all. By these
hick town cops! They wouldn't give me Poppa Hanley's
message!… No, they wouldn't! They told me to go jump m
the lake and they said they didn't believe I was Daffy Dill!
That's just an out for them! You get the idea, don't you?
They want to grab the glory of knocking off the gang and
getting back the kid. They just walk into a setup and they
want the laurel wreath. I'm fighting mad!… Where am

I?... Downstairs in the lobby. I'll be right up.... And I even bought me a rod downtown. A nice big shiny Colt grave-scratcher, a genuine six-shooter some cowhand turned in. It was all primed and ready to go and this happens.—*Wait a second!*—Candid, can you hear me?... Listen... I just saw Pinky Sherman... He went by the lobby desk and got in the elevator—there he goes... He's on his way up! Listen, pal, take it easy. I think he's on his way up to our room! I'm coming up myself. Watch your flesh...."

*(Police Radio Call to El Paso Prowl
Cars, 10:30 A.M. April 3.)*

... Calling car sixty-three... calling sixty-three... proceed at once to Hotel Gunnyson... gun fight in Room 413... man seriously wounded... calling sixty-three...

(Radio Bulletin: Station KXX, El Paso, 11 A.M. April 3.)
FLASH! WE INTERRUPT this broadcast to bring you a special newscast. Flash! Pinky Sherman, notorious killer in the Black Benny Dorgan gang which kidnaped Edith Temple, was shot and killed at the Hotel Gunnyson thirty minutes ago. According to George Gunnyson, manager of the hotel, Pinky Sherman attempted to enter a room engaged by Candid Jones and Daffy Dill. Sherman, feeling that Jones and Dill were too close on the trail of the child, was going to kill them both and cover the gang's trail. Daffy Dill, however, saw Sherman go upstairs and followed him with a gun, having called Candid Jones on the phone to warn him. Sherman went into the room shooting, missed Jones and took a shot at Dill behind him. Jones then fired five bullets into Sherman's body. It was thought at first that

Dill was gravely wounded, but at the Damatian Hospital it was disclosed that the bullet had merely creased his head and knocked him out… Kindly read your daily newspaper for details…

The El Paso Evening Clarion, April 3.
DORGAN GANG ESCAPES FROM POLICE TRAP!
ABDUCTORS FLEE WITH MICH. CHILD
(Copyrighted 1937)

Black Benny Dorgan, brains of the sinister Dorgan gang which snatched Edith Temple on March 31st, escaped from an isolated hideout near the New Mexican border early this afternoon, carrying with him the two-year-old child and the last remaining member of the gang, Machine Gun Jimmy Savell.

It was believed that Dorgan was tipped off by a short wave radio set which was found at the farmhouse. The police informed squad cars by short wave to proceed to the house and Dorgan fled at the alarm…

NA67 THG—WS NEW YORK NY 420P APR 3
DAFFY DILL
HOTEL GUNNYSON
EL PASO TEX
A FINE NEWSPAPERMAN YOU TURNED OUT TO BE STOP WHY DON'T YOU GIVE YOUR-SELF UP STOP SCOOPED AGAIN STOP IT'S GETTING TO BE A HABIT WITH YOU SO I'M NOT SURPRISED THE OLD MAN 427P

NL98 JH—SWE EL PASO TEX 500P APR 3
COLLECT
CITY EDITOR
NEW YORK CHRONICLE
NEW YORK NY
ONE MORE PEEP OUT OF YOU AND I'LL PROM-
ISE TO KNOCK YOUR BLOCK OFF THE FIRST
AND LAST TIME WE MEET STOP HOW DO
YOU EXPECT A GUY TO REPORT A STORY
WHEN HE'S OUT COLD FROM TAKING A
SLUG ACROSS THE SIDE OF HIS HEAD QUES-
TION MARK YOU'RE THE KIND OF GUY WHO
DROWNS BABY DUCKS STOP NOW LAY OFF OR
ELSE CANDID JONES 510P

Hospital Discharge

Patient: Daffy Dill. *Address:* 45 ½ West 45th Street, New York, N.Y. *Admitted to hospital:* April 3rd, 10:45 A.M. *Case:* Gunshot wound on left temple. *Remarks:* Bullet made four inch furrow flesh wound. Patient unconscious for two hours. Responded readily to treatment. Six stitches in wound. Temperature 101 time of admittance. Normal when discharged. Patient asked to be discharged on own responsibility at 5:30 P.M. Discharge granted.

(Signed)

J. Lewis Coxe, M.D.

Attending Physician

NA23 RMX—LP NEW YORK NY 1002P APR 3
DAFFY DILL
HOTEL GUNNYSON

EL PASO TEX
GET IN TOUCH WITH ME PRONTO POPPA
HANLEY 1006P

"HELLO? LISTEN, MY young Texan telephone operator, I'm calling long distance. The name is Daffy Dill, the
destination is the New York Homicide Bureau, the desire
is that you make it as snappy as possible… Ah me, what
a head. Gosh, Candid, it feels like a balloon!… Hello?
Hello! Is that you, Poppa?… How are you? Oh, I'm O.K.
Me and bullets always agree, you know that…. I got your
wire and I called right away. And listen, no more of that
teletype stuff. Those lunkheads pulled a phoney on me
and tried to take Black Benny Dorgan all by themselves.
Did they botch it! Imagine putting a call out to radio cars!
And Dorgan heard them a mile off. I don't know where
he is now and neither does anybody else…. *What? You
do?*… Candid, Poppa says he knows where Black Benny
Dorgan is heading. Hold your hat, we'll be leaving… Go
on, Poppa… Yeah… Yeah… Well, I'll be damned! Just
a second, Poppa. Listen, Candid. Poppa says that Black
Benny was picked up in 1926 on suspicion of having lifted
the Mogul Diamond. Maybe you remember—you do?
Well, Poppa says that Black Benny's alibi was that he had
been at the Two Bar X Ranch twenty miles east of Needles,
California, at a small town named Yucca. Poppa says it's a
regular gangster's haven—you know—like that hotel dive
in Hot Springs, Arkansas?… Hello, Poppa? What do you
suggest this time?… Uh-huh. They went by car no doubt
but we may be wrong…. Uh-huh. If we take a plane and
get there first—I get it, I get it. Okay, Poppa. Thanks a
million. We'll see you in the only city in the world in a

couple of days. Candid says to remember him to Rentano. So long, Poppa!"

NA56 TYU—LS NEW YORK NY 1030P APR 3
CANDID JONES
HOTEL GUNNYSON
EL PASO TEX
PLEASE TAKE CARE OF DAFFY AND SEE THAT HE DOESN'T GET SHOT AGAIN STOP I'M DEPENDING ON YOU DINAH MASON 1035P

NA58 TYU—LA NEW YORK NY 1034R APR 3
CANDID JONES
HOTEL GUNNYSON
EL PASO TEX
WILL PAY YOU A GRAND IF YOU BRING BACK FOTO OF BLACK BENNY DORGAN IN ACTION STOP WILL ALSO LAY OFF DAFFY AS REQUESTED STOP HOW ABOUT IT QUESTION MARK THE OLD MAN 1040P

NA34 FGH—MH EL PASO TEX 1035P APR 3
CITY EDITOR
NEW YORK CHRONICLE
NEW YORK NY
HAVE ALREADY PROMISED CANDID TWO GRAND FOR FOTO YOU CHEAPSKATE STOP TELL DINAH SHE'S CRAZY ABOUT ME STOP YOU'LL HAVE YOUR STORY BEFORE NOON TOMORROW OR ELSE DAFFY 1039P

F-L-A-S-H
LAS CRUCES, N.M.-(AP)—TEMPLE KIDNAPERS
KILL STATION ATTENDANT

B-U-L-L-E-T-I-N S-U-B F-L-A-S-H
LAS CRUCES, NEW MEX. APRIL 3: TWO MEN,
BELIEVED TO BE BLACK BENNY DORGAN AND
MACHINE GUN JIMMY SAVELL, SHOT AND
KILLED A GAS STATION ATTENDANT ON THE
SANTA FE TRAIL NEAR HERE TODAY.
THE GANGSTERS WERE HEADING WEST.
LAS CRUCES POLICE BELIEVE THE MURDER
WAS COMMITTED TO PREVENT IDENTIFICA-
TION AFTER THE MEN HAD STOPPED FOR
GAS. JAMES MORRELO, A SHOE SALESMAN,
PULLED INTO THE STATION JUST AS THE TWO
MEN ROARED OFF IN A BLACK CADILLAC. HE
FOUND THE ATTENDANT'S BODY, IDENTI-
FIED LATER AS JOHN MARX, AND NOTIFIED
THE POLICE. (MORE TO COME.)

"HELLO? HELLO, IS this El Paso airport? This is Candid Jones at the Hotel Gunnyson… Yes… I want to charter a fast cabin plane for two people to fly to Yucca, Arizona, immediately… You have. Good. We'll be right over."

*(Radio Bulletin: Station WEXX, Phoe-
nix, Arizona, 11 P.M. April 3.)*

YOUR RADIO NEWSMAN is on the air again to bring to you the latest news flashes from coast to coast… El Paso, Texas: G-men have chartered a plane and are making ready to fly west on the trail of Black Benny Dorgan and Machine

Gun Jimmy Savell, kidnapers of little Ruth Temple. Dan Purman, chief of the Federal western division, believes that Dorgan is planning to hide out somewhere in the desert. All state police have been notified and a dragnet is being spread to cover all main highways.... Ann Arbor, Michigan: Mrs. Al Temple collapsed here tonight when told by police that there was little hope of finding her two-year-old daughter alive. Police are of the opinion that Dorgan and Savell have slain the girl and hidden the body rather than be hindered in their escape by her presence.

Flash! Here's a last minute news bulletin which just came in hot off the wire. *Flash!* Black Benny Dorgan and Machine Gun Jimmy Savell are in Arizona! They broke across the state line at nine thirty tonight and killed two state policemen in a running gun battle at the border station. The police were killed by machine gun bullets believed to have been fired by Jimmy Savell. The gangsters' black Cadillac was found deserted fifteen minutes later, indicating that they took another car by force and are still heading west. There was no sign of Edith Temple in the deserted Cadillac....

"HELLO... GET ME the New York Chronicle.... Hello, is this the Old Man?... This is Poppa Hanley down at h.q. I've been sitting at this desk all night with Rentano, chewing my fingernails. We wondered if you'd had any word from either Daffy or Candid.... You haven't heard? Hell.... They should have been at Yucca hours ago. It's six P.M. *now*... Okay, then. Give us a ring when you hear anything...."

"HELLO, POLICE HEADQUARTERS? This is Al Temple speaking. The missus is feeling pretty bad boys, and she

asked me to give you a buzz again. Have you had any word
yet? You ain't?... Well... Sure, boys, sure, I know you're
doing your best....If I could just wrap these hands around
that dirty little rat's throat—Dorgan I mean. Yeah, yeah,
you're right. That don't do no good... Well... Look, boys,
gimme a ring the first thing you hear from the west, heh?
Thanks a helluva lot, boys...."

(Radio Broadcast: Station KXEX
Los Angeles, 9 A.M. April 4.)

STRANGE, UNCANNY SILENCE has settled upon the
Temple kidnaping. There have been no new developments since it was established that Black Benny Dorgan
had entered Arizona. His trail seems to have been lost
completely. It is believed that Dorgan and Machine Gun
Jimmy Savell are heading for the California border. All
state police have been asked to guard all entry places and
the Los Angeles police have erected a barricade at Blythe.
Fixed machine guns are ready to rake any car which does
not stop at the border when signalled. Repercussions of
the incident in El Paso yesterday....

NA23 TR—EM NEEDLES CAL 1001A APR 4
CITY EDITOR
NEW YORK CHRONICLE
NEW YORK NY
FLASH STOP WE KILLED SAVELL STOP
CAPTURED DORGAN STOP RESCUED EDITH
STOP STORY FOLLOWS STOP PIX GOING BY
WIRE DAFFY 1005A

(The New York Chronicle, Noon Stocks Edition, April 4.)

EXTRA!

EDITH SAFE!

DORGAN CAPTURED!

SAVELL KILLED IN GUN BATTLE WITH

REPORTER

Daffy Dill and Candid Jones Hire Plane to Trap Kidnapers
on Desert

CHILD IS ALIVE

Exclusive to the New York Chronicle

BY DAFFY DILL

(See Special Wirephotos on Page 5)

NEEDLES, CALIF. April 4: We found Edith Temple safe
and sound in the dawn of a desert day on the Arizona border
this morning. By we I mean a gentleman named Candid
Jones and myself. We not only found Edith Temple, we also
found Machine Gun Jimmy Savell and Black Benny Dorgan.
And when the smoke had cleared away, Jimmy Savell was
dead....

Needles, California
April 4
Via Air Mail

Lt. William Hanley
New York Homicide Bureau
Centre Street
New York, N.Y.

MY VERY OWN fran, Poppa:

Undoubtedly you are reading all the hooey in the Chronicle at the moment. That's why I'm writing to tell you the

whole yarn. No matter how you write it a newspaper story is still a newspaper story and you have to leave out some things and put in others. So here goes the opus. Hang on.

Your tip last night in El Paso was hot stuff. Poppa, you can be very proud of having hit the nail on the nose.

Right after you called, Candid chartered a four place Cinna monoplane, a nice little red job. It cost us five hundred bucks. We went down to the airport around midnight and we met the pilot, a nice enough guy named Phil Merry.

"Where bound, gents?" Merry said when we got in.

"Yucca," I said. "Can you make a night landing?"

"I've got flares," said Merry. "We can make a landing easy there. They got a stretch of desert cleared off. Emergency landing field for VTH Lines, you know, the transcontinental ships."

Candid said: "And don't spare the horses. We're in a hell of a hurry."

"What'd you say your names were?" Merry asked, peering.

"We didn't say," I said, "but since you ask they're Daffy Dill and Candid Jones."

"Why," Merry said then, "you two guys are chasing the Temple snatchers!"

"Right the first time," I said. "Shall we away?"

We awayed all right. It got under Merry's skin and he was a right guy. Gosh, Poppa, he didn't even want to get paid when he learned we were after those two rats. He took us up to 15,000 feet and we stayed there all the way, hell bent for leather. That ship could fly and Merry made it do tricks.

Now Merry had a short wave radio set in his ship and he gave us an idea how to work the contraption and Candid and I listened in to hear what we could hear. Pretty soon the amateurs started buzzing back and forth and—what a break for us—two of them got hot on the Temple kidnaping. They started talking about how Dorgan and Savell had switched cars, how they'd got into Arizona.

Along about five A.M. when the sun was coming up back of us nice and red like your nose after three drinks, Candid got a flash on the short wave set that nearly knocked him over. And that guy is a pretty cool customer, let me tell you.

"Daffy," he said, "get this. Black Benny knocked off another gas station guy no more than an hour ago. But the guy lived to tell the tale. He said they were in a gray Buick and heading for Cross Mountain near Sandy Creek... Ask Merry where we are now."

I tapped Merry on the shoulder and gave him the business.

"We've been running behind time," Merry said. "A couple of head winds here haven't been any help. We just passed Rock Butte ten minutes ago. I can pick up the Cross Mountain road easily if you say the word. Daylight's due to break anyhow. There's the sun."

I said: "Do that little thing, Merry."

Those mountains didn't look too nice for landings. Arizona is a funny state, Poppa. It's got the flattest deserts, the biggest rivers and dams, the nicest cattle country and the damnedest crags and canyons you ever laid a glimmer on.

About twenty minutes later on the other side of Cross Mountain going downhill toward Yucca, we picked out a lone car traveling like the wind. We didn't come down much for two reasons: mountains and not wanting Dorgan to be suspicious of the ship. But we could see that car plain as day. It still had headlights on and it was gray. The sun was up pretty well then.

"Well," Merry said, "those guys have got to go across the Mongo Desert west of Cross Mountain. It's a flat lake bed about ten miles long but there's one part they call the Devil's Floor where the highway passes through a maze of petrified stalactites. What I mean is, a car has to stay on the road. If it touched those stalactites, the tires would blow out and the car would be tossed all to hell."

Candid nodded as though he understood but I didn't get it.

"How come?" I asked. "What's the bee in your fedora?"

"Why," Merry replied, "it's a nice highway. I'll beat them there in the ship and I'll land on the highway. There are no poles no wires, no nothing. Then I'll taxi the ship around facing them and kick over the prop. They can do three things. Hit a whirling prop head on, hit the stalactites and crash, or stop. My comrades, I have seen the Devil's Floor and you can take my word for it—they'll stop."

"No sooner said than done," I said. "Descend, Merry."

MY TICKER WAS rubbing against my Adam's apple on that landing. The roadway looked like a strip of toothpaste when we tried to land on it. But this Merry was O.K. and he set her down with nary a jitter and we finally taxied to a stop. He jazzed the engine and shot the tail around to face east on the highway.

"No," Candid said. "They could sneak by under a wing maybe. Stick her right across the lanes."

So we parked the monoplane right on the highway north and south so that a streamlined eel couldn't have passed on either side without going off into the Devil's Floor.

And this Devil's Floor was well named. A pack of sharp knife-like spears sticking straight up off the lake bed like a bad dream. Solid rock, they were, and very nasty.

"I give them ten minutes," Candid Jones said. "How about it, Daffy?"

"I don't know," I shrugged.

"Just about that," said Merry. "They ought to be down the mountain now."

We got out of the ship. I took out my Colt .31 grave-scratcher, the original ole six-shooter and I made ready to start fanning the hammer. Candid got out his Lüger 9 mm and his Leica camera and Merry went back to the plane and got out a 20 gauge doublebarrelled shot-gun which he used to go coyote hunting from the plane with. This six-shooter I have is something, Poppa. I got it in El Paso and I'll give you a look when I get home again.

I said: "Candid, I'm going down the line about thirty feet and park the carcass behind one of them Devil's toothpicks. That way, I'll cover them from behind."

Candid said: "Good, Daffy. I'll go down about fifteen feet and cover them from the opposite side."

"How about me?" Merry asked.

"You want to be in on this?"

"Definitely," Merry said.

"Then you stand—no—get in the plane for cover and stick that riot gun out the window. If things go wrong, let 'em have it where it'll kill," Candid said quietly.

"No," I said. "You can kill Savell if you want but let's

bring Dorgan in alive so there won't be any lynch law stuff in this."

Candid laughed coldly. "Lynch law? When those rats have a machine gun?"

"I know," I said. "But I think the G-men and the cops would like to have Dorgan to work on."

"O.K.," Candid said. "Let's go."

We went down the road. I found me a nice toothpick of rock and hid behind it and took a look for Candid but I couldn't find him anywhere. I saw Merry climb into the plane and I saw the maw of that shotgun cover the road.

It couldn't have been more than five minutes later when the gray Buick came highballing around the curve in the road and burst down upon the plane.

Black Benny Dorgan was driving and I never saw a guy look so surprised as when Dorgan saw that monoplane parked across the road. He started to swing around it and saw the stalactites. Then he jammed on the brakes and skidded to a harrowing stop, spinning half around.

He knew the jig was up. He came out of the car running fast for cover. Machine Gun Jimmy Savell came out on Candid's side, running low and firing a Tommy gun at nothing in particular. Inside the car, Edith Temple was crying, "Momma, momma!"

I came out from behind the toothpick and went after Dorgan. Over on Candid's side, the submachine gun began to keep a steady chatter and the slugs were slapping against the rocks. I heard the roar of the Lüger twice and then a terrific explosion. I realized that Merry had fired the shotgun.

The submachine gun stopped chattering. When I

reached the highway I saw Jimmy Savell dead there, nearly torn in half from the buckshot, and two slug holes in his head from Candid's pistol.

Candid came running after Dorgan from the other side and we both closed on Black Benny, who whirled around, firing a series of wild shots at us which came close but no cigar, if you get me. Candid yelled to Merry not to use the other barrel on Dorgan.

"Daffy!" Candid cried then. "You take Benny! I've got to get a photo for the Old Man!"

Benny stopped running and turned to make a stand and I let him have one low with the Colt gravescratcher. I hit him in the left knee by luck and the slug knocked him flat on his back.

"Great!" Candid yelled. "Caught him falling!" He had the candid camera up to his eye and was shooting pictures for all he was worth, his Lüger hanging in his other hand.

When Benny fell, I dove on top of him and I began to wallop him with everything I had, including the barrel of the gravescratcher. Candid finally pulled me off the ginzo and said: "For God's sake, Daffy, you were the guy who wanted him alive. Lay off. I think you've busted his skull. You clubbed him long enough for me to take eight pictures."

And that was the works.

We put the kid in the plane. Candid piled Dorgan and Savell back into the car and drove it. Then I flew off with Merry for Needles to get the story on the wire and have Candid's film developed.

By the time Candid reached Needles, the fotos had been developed. I put them back on the plane and Merry flew to Los Angeles and had them wired to the Chronicle by Associated Press Wirephoto Service. I parked in the Needles telegraph office and wrote my story and sent it off to the Old Man and it didn't take long before G-men were there in quantities and Edith Temple was in custody for return to her parents. I had to answer a lot of questions, my fran.

So that's the dope. Take it easy, many thanks, and I'll see you soon, Poppa.

Yours in haste,
Daffy.

NA56 HJK—LK NEW YORK NY 200P APR 4
DAFFY DILL
NEEDLES CALIF
SCOOPED THE NATION STOP BEST JOB OF
YOUR CAREER STOP CONGRATS THE OLD
MAN 210P

NA67 YUI—P ANN ARBOR MICH 240P APR 4
DAFFY DILL & CANDID JONES
NEEDLES CALIF
MAYBE I'VE HAD YOU GUYS WRONG ALL MY
LIFE STOP ANYWAY THANKS AL TEMPLE 245P

NA54 DFS—MH NEW YORK NY 247P APR 4
DAFFY DILL
NEEDLES CALIF
ALL IS FORGIVEN STOP COME HOME TO
GARBO DINAH 250P

NA99 DSA—QW NEEDLES CALIF 300P APR 4
DINAH MASON
NEW YORK CHRONICLE
NEW YORK NY
FAIR WEATHER FRIEND HAH QUESTION
MARK CANDID AND I ARE CATCHING THE
SANTA FE CHIEF TODAY FOR HOLLYWOOD
TO SEE THE REAL GARBO STOP WE'LL BE
HOME MAYBE IN A COUPLE OF WEEKS STOP
MEANWHILE THE CROWD WILL KINDLY
STAND BACK STOP CALIFORNIA HERE I COME
DAFFY 310P

www.ingramcontent.com/pod-product-compliance
Lightning Source LLC
Chambersburg PA
CBHW072352030726
47505CB00014B/1765